A SIDEKICK'S TALE

A
SIDEKICK'S
TALE

ELISABETH GRACE FOLEY

Illustrations by Annie Grubb

Cover design by Jennifer Zemanek/Seedlings Design Studio

ISBN: 1979206740
ISBN-13: 978-1979206747

TABLE OF CONTENTS

CHAPTER ONE

Meredith Fayett
Makes A Proposal

THE TROUBLE began with a mortgage, which shouldn't be taken lightly any more than a marriage. And if any of you think marriage should be taken lightly—well, you'll find out, that's all. That's the whole moral of the story right there, really, but since people generally prefer the story to the moral, I suppose I'd better let you have the whole thing.

I wasn't the principal player in it, but if it hadn't of been for me none of it would have happened, which is saying something. There's lots of fellows whose names don't get into the history books, but if they hadn't been there at the other fellow's elbow at the right moment, the world would have—well, either have missed out on something sensational or been spared a lot of grief, I don't know which. I'll leave it to you to decide what I contributed.

There had to be a woman in the case, of course. Search for a female, as the French say. Meredith Fayett didn't even look grown-up enough to be called a woman the first time I saw her. That was in—oh, ninety-seven or ninety-eight, a few years before the story really begins. Before the *Maine* blew up. She was just a bit of a girl with red-gold hair and a pretty smile who used to come down from St. Louis with her aunt for a few weeks in the summer. The old lady owned the Fayett ranch, which didn't fit her too well—it let in too much fresh air at the seams—but that wasn't her fault because it had come to her from a late older brother she didn't get along with. But her niece liked the outdoors and she liked her niece, so she endured the outdoors. The ranch was a nice little place—small, I'll grant, but it had a white frame house with creeping vines all over the front porch, and grew good crops of imported cattle and native alfalfa. Not a showpiece, but the barns didn't leak and the house had been brought up to date with an icebox and screen doors and such.

Well, when the old lady died of a surplus of years the ranch came to Meredith Fayett. She came to the ranch about a month later, since she had always preferred it to St. Louis, and set right in learning how to manage the place. She learned quick and didn't pester the lives out of us with foolish questions, neither. There was half a dozen of us working there, and during the old lady's time we'd been mostly left to our own devices, though since the last foreman left Chance Stevens had been more or less in charge. We all thought for a lady boss, Meredith Fayett was all right—before long there wasn't a one of us who wouldn't have stood on his head if he thought it would do her some good.

She ended up asking for something a little more difficult.

One day when she'd been at the ranch for a couple of months, the banker in Culver's Corners asked her to drop by his office. When she got there she found it wasn't to take afternoon tea but to hear some startling financial facts. It seems a city lawyer had had the job of juggling her aunt's investments and shares and salaries by long distance, and neither he nor Aunt had bothered much with the ranch. The brother beforehand had left the place mortgaged to the neck, and the Aunt preferred to spend as little of her income as possible on paying it off. So Banker Ross explained to Meredith Fayett that if she couldn't put a lump sum on those back-payments right off, she'd lose the place in about a week.

I could tell she had something bothering her when she got back from town. She'd really come to love that place, and the idea of it going at auction wasn't a pleasant one. She'd ridden to town and back, and she gave her horse to one of the boys to take care of and walked over to the house, twisting her quirt in her hands and wearing a little frown that was almost as pretty as her smile. She went up on the front porch, which ran along the front of the house and round the corner, and walked along it slowly till she came abreast of where Chance Stevens and I were unsaddling our horses near the yard pump on the other side of the railing. It's something to think, you know, that if we'd unsaddled in the barn that day I might not be telling this story at all. Just goes to show you it's the little things that count after all.

She wasn't looking at us to begin with; we were just there; but then her eyes widened a little like she'd got an idea, and it was Chance her eyes were on. I don't know why she picked him. All the boys were pretty decent upstanding fellows. I suppose it was because he was young and fairly good-looking, while the rest of us were over thirty and there wasn't any artist who was going to ask to paint our pictures.

I could tell that whatever idea had come to her, it was the kind that scares you a little at first, because it's so big you wonder how you could be the one to think of it. Then her face changed so I could see she was getting used to it, getting to the point where you begin to think it might actually work. It's right about then that some people just blurt it out, before they've had a chance to think it over a second time and have second thoughts. That's what Meredith did.

She put her hands on the railing and leaned over it. "Chance, could you do me a favor?"

He looked up quick and smiled at her. "Sure, Miss Meredith. What's the trouble?"

"Would you—could you marry me?"

Chance was just bending down on the other side of his horse as she spoke, and he popped up and gave her a look across the saddle to make sure he'd heard what he thought he did. "What?"

"Well, not really. I mean, yes, really. But it wouldn't be—I mean, you wouldn't have to—" She turned about as pink as a June rose and stuck for a minute.

"Miss Meredith, are you—are you feeling all right?" said Chance, looking at her kind of concerned, and you couldn't blame him.

"Oh, yes, I'm all right," she said, smiling and looking a little embarrassed. "But I've got to be married before next Friday or I'm going to lose the ranch."

That didn't sound any saner to me. But Meredith Fayett was dead in earnest. She got up on the porch rail and sat there with her back to the post and explained it all, and Chance leaned his folded arms over his saddle and listened to her. She made an awfully pretty picture perched up there with the greenery hanging down behind her, swinging one little riding-boot back and forth as she talked. She looked like a sweet innocent little girl, and let me tell you, there had to be a fair amount of little girl left in any woman who could make a proposal like this and make it seriously.

"I never knew this property was mortgaged until recently. My father left me some money in trust that would help pay it off, but I can't touch the capital until I come of age or marry. The interest isn't enough to pay what's due on the mortgage—and I won't be twenty-one for six months. So I thought—if I could find someone to marry me—only on paper, you understand. I only thought I'd ask you, but of course you needn't do it if you'd rather not. I just thought…"

She stopped, and sighed. I suppose she thought

it was really too ridiculous and the ranch was as good as gone—and I agreed with her. The story of the pretty girl who's going to lose the ranch is as old as barbed wire, but this adaptation was a new one on me and not likely to catch on with the public.

Chance pushed his hat back on his forehead. He was the sort who grasps things much too quickly—you know, the ones who can blurt out the answer to the arithmetic problem before you've got through reading it—which had frustrated me many a time before. But when he spoke I inwardly blessed my comparative slow-wittedness. Better slow than sorry, as the saying goes.

He said, "Well, no—I understand. I'd like to help you if I can…"

"It would only be for a few months," said Meredith hopefully, "and it wouldn't really *mean* anything. Unless—unless there's another girl, or something of that sort—"

"No—no," said Chance, looking almost as embarrassed as she did.

"And you needn't worry about losing your job here. I suppose you can come back and work here just the same after you've abandoned me."

"Hold up. When did I do that?" said Chance.

"That's what's required in order to get an annulment, afterwards," said Meredith. "It's a legal term," she added, the way people do when they're not quite sure what something means themselves.

She added hesitantly, "I could make it worth your while—if you'd like a raise in your pay, or—"

That did it. Chance was the high-spirited, sensitive kind that get offended when you mention money within a day's march of something personal, and marriage is nothing if not personal. He stiffened up right away, frowning. "The last time I did somebody a favor I didn't ask to get paid for it," he said shortly. "I don't want any money. I'll do it. I'm glad to help you out."

"Oh, thank you," she said, breaking into that smile of hers, and you could tell that even though she'd been too shy to push a delicate question like proposing marriage to a fellow, she really wanted to keep that ranch. Chance brightened up like a mirror when you smile into it, and I couldn't blame him for that, either. Meredith's smile was more worth seeing than whatever most people meet there.

"When do you want to do it?" he asked.

She gave it a second's thought. "Well, would tomorrow do? I want to take care of those payments as soon as I can. Tomorrow afternoon?"

"All right by me. Any time you say."

All this time I'd been close by, watching like I was at a performance, and not entirely sure it *wasn't* an opera of some kind by how improbable it was. Once Meredith Fayett had gone into the house I got out of the audience and let Chance Stevens have it good.

"I've witnessed some colossal pieces of impulse in my time," said I, "but this one takes the cake. And I had you figured for a smart kid. I'll bet you didn't know that," I added, which was probably true. I don't believe in flattery.

Chance looked at me blankly, like he'd forgotten I was there, which he probably had. That happened sometimes when Meredith and I were both in the vicinity. Then he gave me a funny patronizing smile, like a man does whenever he's mixed up with a woman and feels like he knows more about her than you ever could, and shrugged. "Aw, it's nothing much."

"You're the first man I ever heard describe marriage as 'nothing much'."

Chance only laughed at me. "But Marty, it isn't really *marriage*," he said. "Didn't you hear anything she said? It's just on paper."

"I've got ears, and I've got eyes, and I'm reasonably sure I've got brains," said I. "I admit no bachelor can be rightly regarded as an expert on matrimony, even if he's a minister, because his expertness doesn't even extend as far as the honeymoon, which is a poor example in itself. But—"

"What are you talking about?" demanded Chance, who had been left even further behind than the marriage license, judging from the look on his face. I wondered how I could ever have appraised anyone who could look that foolish as a 'smart kid.'

"Suffering sassafras!" said I, out of patience. "Listen here, Chance. I come from a large family, with plenty of women in it. Nine aunts and uncles—I mean nine pairs of them—besides my own folks, not to mention girl cousins and so on. I'm not against the married state, but I can say from secondhand experience it's nothing to go into with your eyes shut and your hands tied behind your back."

Chance didn't seem to care. He just laughed again as he loosened the cinch and slid the saddle off his horse. "I told you, it's not *really* marriage, the way we're doing it."

I shook my head. "Marriage is marriage, no matter how many times you two keep saying 'not really' like it's some kind of hocus-pocus."

"Oh, shut up," said Chance good-naturedly. "I'm doing a lady a favor, that's all; I'm not going to get in trouble. She's square; she'll do like she said and it'll all be over in a few months."

"It's too good to be true," I said gloomily, as I pulled the headstall over my horse's ears. "I'm no legal *or* matrimonial expert, but you mark my words, sonny boy, there's going to be a catch in it somewhere."

Which there was, of course, though it wasn't at all what I expected it to be.

Chapter Two

Clinching the Deal

HAVING SEEN the first act, I made sure I was on the spot when the curtain went up on the second one. You see, at this point I still thought it was free admission...but I'm getting ahead of myself.

Anyway, it wasn't hard for me to tag along when Chance Stevens and Meredith Fayett rode into Culver's Corners together the next afternoon. We didn't look much like a wedding party. She had on her riding togs with the middy blouse and tie and the wide-brimmed hat she always wore outdoors, and Chance the same old blue shirt he wore every day — and me, I never was one for formal attire even on special occasions.

We reined up in front of the Justice of the Peace's little office. "You'd better come in, Marty; we might need you for a witness," said Chance as we dismounted.

"I'm not prepared to stand the damages if the

deal falls through," said I, "but I'll come along and lend moral support. You'll need it."

"Oh, shut up," he said, friendly as ever.

The Justice of the Peace was a fat bald little man with cheeks like apples and fingers like sausages. Taken altogether he'd have kept a whole tribe of cannibals happy for a week. He was a cheerful kind of creature too; he greeted Meredith like a long-lost daughter. She explained that she'd come to be married.

"Oh, then you've found one!" said the Justice of the Peace.

It seems the Justice of the Peace had fore-gathered with Banker Ross shortly after the man of money delivered his broadside to Meredith, and Ross had told him how Meredith needed to take a matrimonial partner into the firm by Friday or go bust—to prepare him for a visit at Thursday midnight if the search went down to the wire, I suppose. The Justice, who you might say had both a friendly and a professional interest in the case, was happy to find she'd succeeded.

"Well, shall we get down to business?" he said, rubbing his fat hands together and looking at Chance and me. "Which one of them is it?"

I withdrew myself from the running and re-treated to a chair by the wall that offered a good view; in the dress-circle, you might say. The J. of the P. gets out a paper and busies himself with officialness. "Your full names, please."

"Chance Alexander Stevens," says the afore-mentioned a little stiffly.

("Alexander!" says I to myself with a chuckle.)

"Meredith Clarice Fayett," said she, quiet and cool. She'd begun to look a little pale and starry-eyed, just as if it was the real thing. To a woman a wedding is a wedding, with or without the trimmings.

The J. of the P. arranged himself behind the desk with his little book in both hands while they stood side by side opposite, and he sort of threw back his head and puffed out his chest and commenced reading in a pompous voice, enjoying every second of it. "Dearly beloved, we are gathered here today to join together this man and this woman in holy matrimony. You may now kiss the bride."

Chance and the girl both kind of jumped and threw a scared look at each other. The J. of the P. gave a foolish giggle. "Oh, excuse me. I skipped a page."

Both of them *looked* a sigh of relief, although you couldn't hear anything, and settled down again. But Chance tugged uneasily at his neckerchief. He was starting to sweat a little.

The J. of the P. had wound himself up again

and was rolling on. "Do you, Chance, take this woman to be your lawful wedded wife, to love and to cher—to, er—hmmm...let's see..."

He frowned at the book. The discrepancy between the ceremony and the circumstances was holding him up a little.

He tried again. "Let's put it this way: Do you, Chance, promise to adhere to whatever agreement you two have settled between yourselves, for as long as ye both shall deem it necessary?"

He had imagination, that little judge.

"Sure," said Chance. He didn't.

"Do you, Meredith, take this man to be your lawful wedded husband, promising to comply with the terms and conditions of said agreement, for better or worse?"

By this time I think he'd forgotten whether he was assisting at a marriage or conspiring at a mortgage.

"I do," said Meredith, quiet like before. She hadn't.

"And now the ring!" said the J. of the P. brightly.

"Oh," said Meredith, looking distressed. She looked up at Chance and over at the Justice. "We forgot about that. Do we need to have one?"

"Well, it isn't—so far as I know—required by law," said the J., "but I always recommend it. It adds a certain stamp of—shall we say respectability?—to the proceedings." The Justice was evidently a fellow who took some pride in his work. He wasn't one for doing things halfway.

That was when I had my brilliant inspiration.

"Hey!" I said. I sprang up from the witness-chair and began digging in my pockets as I made my way up to the altar. "I've got something here that might work."

I held it out to Meredith. It was no slouch of a ring, either. It was real gold, I think, though a little tarnished, and the green stone in the middle still sparkled nice after quite a while down in my pocket. It looked a lot better out where the light could get to it. Meredith gave a kind of "ohhhh" and took it pretty near reverently. "It's beautiful, Marty," she said. "It looks old, too. It must be an heirloom."

"It was my grandmother's," I said with satisfaction.

That touched her even more. "Are you sure you want to give it away? No, you ought to keep it," she said, trying to hand it back to me.

"No, no, you go ahead and use it. I've been carrying that around a long time—always figured I'd find the right girl to give it to someday," I said, chuckling at my own joke.

The Justice of the Peace shook his fat cheeks a little, like he was trying to clear a muddled head. "I really am getting too old for this sort of thing," said he to himself.

I didn't catch on until Chance elbowed me, and then I realized I was breaking up the J.'s field of vision, right there between the bride and groom. I sidestepped and came up on Chance's right. Meredith had already slipped the ring on her finger and was sort of brooding over it. The J. of the P. perked up again and rolled out the concluding paragraph: "So, by the powers vested in me by the State of Missouri, I pronounce you man and wife, to all legal intents and purposes. And here we are on page twenty-seven again," he added, with another giggle.

They were beginning to look uncomfortable again, but the ever-resourceful Justice, who was the only one to see the humor in that particular clause of the ceremony, came to the rescue. "Sometimes the letter of the law is not—well, what's required here is a tangible token of both parties' willingness to seal the agreement. I suppose shaking hands would do."

"Works to clinch most deals," I said.

They followed his suggestion, and Meredith held on to Chance's hand for a minute and looked up into his face. "Thank you," she said softly, and you could see just how grateful she was.

"Don't mention it," said Chance, with a rather foolish smile.

"Case dismissed," added the Justice of the Peace.

He shook hands with us all around, and gave Meredith a copy of the marriage certificate—to show the bank she hadn't taken any shortcuts, I suppose. Once she got that she was all in a flutter, and told Chance she wanted to go over to the bank right away and make sure they wired her father's lawyer in time. So she said goodbye to the Justice and went out ahead of us.

When we were out on the porch, and she was out of sight, Chance drew his sleeve across his forehead and blew out a deep breath, like a man who's just escaped from a hot room. The J.'s office hadn't been particularly stifling.

"Well, that wasn't so bad after all," I said with what was supposed to be killing irony. "Really nothing to it, is there?"

"Oh, shut up," said Chance, but without his usual friendliness.

Chapter Three

One Thing Leads To Another

W E MET Meredith coming back from the bank, a happy uplifted look on her face. The ring on her hand flashed when the sun hit it, and I remarked to myself that it did go nice with her complexion. One good thing that had come out of that day's work, at least.

"It's all right," she said. "The payment will be made as soon as the money is wired down here. I'm so relieved; I don't know how to thank you, Chance."

Then Chance said something that sounded kind of impertinent, but made me look at him like he was a whole lot smarter than I'd had him figured for. I began to think that Meredith Fayett—excuse me, Meredith Stevens—could have done worse.

He said, "If you're planning to sink a big chunk of that trust on the mortgage, what are you going to live on? There won't be much interest off what's left."

Meredith nodded thoughtfully. "I know. I

talked about that with Mr. Ross when this first came up, and I decided I'd have to choose between the ranch and the income. I don't want to live in the city—and I have a little money my aunt left me. I'll just have to make the ranch pay from now on."

There were a lot of choice remarks jostling each other on my tongue about being willing to commit matrimony just to possess yourself of a little one-horse ranch in an indifferent shape and not overmuch cash to run it with, but I swallowed them untasted.

"Well," said Chance, "if you want to improve the herd, I'd start by culling it down and selling off the odds and ends. You could put a field or two into a cash crop, too; that would help."

"I'll do it!" said Meredith decidedly. "It sounds sensible to me. Why did you never suggest it before, Chance? I've spent all this spring wondering what more could be done with the ranch that wasn't being done."

Chance looked down at the ground and scuffed his boot in the dust. "I'm only a hired hand, Miss Meredith—I didn't figure I had the right to make suggestions without your asking for them."

"Well, I wish you would," said Meredith. "I'll be glad of any suggestions you can make. I'm going to need all the help I can get!" She gave him another rendition of her particular smile.

"After all," I told Chance as we headed back to our horses, "maybe you have a little more right to give advice now. You're not just a hand, you're a husband. But oh, I forgot—not really."

"Oh, shut up," said Chance in a hurry, like he thought Meredith might hear.

A few blocks along the main street, as we rode out of town, we passed the building that Roger Torrance called his office—which the only things he had to support this claim were that it had four walls, a roof, a door and some windows, as offices generally do. What's more, Roger Torrance himself was standing on the front porch. He was supposed to be a surveyor, but I don't know how he made a living at it because I never personally knew him to do a lick of work in his life. He was a young man with smooth black hair who spent his time going about looking smart in suits that looked like they stepped out of a mail-order catalogue, ties too good to be true, a hat tipped at an angle that made you want to knock it the rest of the way off and a charming, supercilious smile that inspired similar thoughts. When I'd been in town with Meredith Fayett a few times before, I'd seen him occupying her vicinity and making himself agreeable, all nods and becks and wreathed smiles. As we passed now, he straightened up from where he'd been artistically leaning against a post and touched his hat to her.

"Good afternoon, Miss Fayett," he said.

Meredith blushed a little. You could tell from the way he said it that Roger Torrance knew she wasn't (strictly speaking) Miss Fayett any longer. In a place like Culver's Corners everybody knows everything about you almost before you know it yourself.

"We haven't seen as much of you in town lately," said Torrance. "I hope your ranch doesn't keep you *too* busy—because the loss is ours."

He tossed an indifferent nod somewhere in the neighborhood between Chance and me, like he'd just happened to notice we were there. I rode on thinking that if I'd been the sort to carry a gun all the time, how I would have liked to put a few slugs on the ground near Torrance's feet and spatter dust all on his pretty new clothes. I had an uncle who taught me that trick once.

I saw Chance throw a disgusted look over his shoulder at him too as we passed. But Meredith just smiled and bowed a little after Torrance spoke to her, and rode on. I think the main reason that kind of bird maddens decent fellows is that they can never understand why women go for it like they do. You'd think any girl with half a grain of sense would know a creature like Torrance isn't worth half the price of his fancy outfit, but even women with more than their fair share of smarts get taken in by his kind every day.

Where was I? Oh. Well, by all rights that should have been the end of the whole affair, at least until after they'd figured out how the abandonment-and-annulment business worked, when there would have been some more officialness and everybody would have been right back where they started. But it wasn't —not by a long shot. And the reasons why not were a study in how one thing leads to another.

The first thing I noticed was how after this, Meredith and Chance got to be friends in an odd kind of way. I suppose being married, even if it's just on paper, has that effect on people. Not that things weren't a little awkward between them at first, of course. I'd never known Chance to trip over his own feet before. To try and imagine what the two of them must be thinking whenever they met made me feel almost as muddled in the head as the old J. of the P.

But they got over that soon enough and became downright companionable. Chance used to hang around the house sometimes in the evenings, and Meredith would come out to the corner of the porch with the vines on it and talk to him. If I happened to be outside I'd hear their voices, and Meredith's laugh, which was as simple and pretty as the rest of her, drifting across the yard in that easy kind of quietness you get around sundown, and look over to see her sitting in the porch swing and Chance leaning against the railing, looking like they were getting along first-rate. They'd talk till far past dusk sometimes. That muddled me even more, but if they were content, I wasn't going to stretch my brain trying to wrap it around the whys and wherefores.

Next came the interest Meredith started to take in raising cattle. Not the old-fashioned way with roundups and branding-irons, but the scientific method of cultivating and grafting them and giving them vitamins and plotting out their geographical bloodlines in a notebook and such. She got books and pamphlets from the livestock societies and read up on the subject, and invested some of the Aunt's legacy in whitewashing the old barns and buying stainless-steel grain buckets (all of which probably would have horrified the Aunt if she'd been around to see it), and she began making some right-smart little deals in new fancy-blooded stock to help with the cultivating. I suppose this was some of what she and Chance used to talk about in the evenings. Like I said, he was a smart boy; he'd been to school and all that and he'd sometimes come out with surprisingly intelligent ideas. I think he was about the closest thing to a congruous combination of an old-time cowpuncher and what they call the Modern Farmer that you'd ever hope to see.

The upshot of this was that the old Fayett place began to really wake up and stretch itself. I'd swear the barns stood up straighter. The new coat of paint didn't bother its antebellum charm, but the scientific methods were being proved in theory to make a pleasant impression on the bank-book. You couldn't exactly have rolled in the accumulated wealth, but you could have sat on it comfortably. And a comfortable chair is about all anyone can ask for. It would suit me. The new order of things suited most everybody pretty well—I say most because one of the hands did quit; he said there were getting to be too many fences for his taste, but I think he really meant too many gates because he was always forgetting to close them and Chance told him that if he didn't develop a taste for remembering he'd assist his memory by—but that's another story. The fellow left, and I got to open and close the gates.

And what all this led to in the end was the cattle-buying trip that Chance and I went on. Meredith had her eye on another batch of experimental livestock, a local recipe cooked up by another scientifically-minded rancher over in the town of Radley Hill, quite a decent distance away, and she wanted Chance to go and take a look at them and see if they were worth considering or just a quack formula. I was going along mainly to keep him company, though I fully intended to shove my oar in if I contracted an opinion of my own. I was generally the fifth wheel to the combine as far as all this Modern Farming was concerned, but life around the Fayett place had been so pleasant lately that I didn't mind.

We got off early one cool morning just as the sun was giving advance notice over behind the hills. This was around three months after the Justice of the Peace had ad-libbed his way through the wedding scene. Meredith came running out of the house just as we had finished saddling up, with a lunch she'd packed for us to take along. She was prettier than ever, and looked to me like she'd grown up a little since she began taking responsibilities into her own hands. And she was still wearing the ring I'd given her. I don't know if it was because she felt she *ought* to, being legally married and all, or if she just liked the ring. Maybe both.

Anyway, she gave Chance the bag of lunch and a few last-minute instructions, which she'd already given him before, of course, and then we said goodbye and mounted up. It was a pretty morning, all right, with the birds singing up in the tops of the trees and everything looking fresh and ready to go, and we were feeling all right and ready to go ourselves. Chance whistled a bit of a tune as we jogged out of the yard. When we got to where the lane bent around the trees to join the road we both turned in our saddles to look back, and Meredith was waving goodbye to us from the porch.

CHAPTER FOUR

Hide and Seek

I T'S NEVER any use to speculate on what might have happened if what *did* happen hadn't happened. For instance, what might have happened if Chance and I had actually reached the laboratory of the scientific rancher. I've thought about it sometimes, but never for long. Because there's probably nothing that could have beaten what *did* happen.

We were several days into our trip and a considerable distance from home. It was kind of a hot day so we were taking it easy, letting our horses amble along. We were on a flat stretch of road with a pretty steep sandy bank sloping down on the right to something between a creek and a river; and on our left a grassy bank sloped up into some trees with long branches that hung down and trailed on the ground. Up ahead the road made a long curve around to the left, and the river or whatever it was followed it around the curve, so we could see the water twinkling right in front of us about half a mile away.

It really was a prime place for an ambush, but of course we weren't thinking about that. Having your mind too much on Modern Farming can make you forget about the primitiveness of Missouri, where they still run to bushwhacking on occasion. At any rate, we were going along when all of a sudden a voice behind us says, "Hold up!"—not threateningly, but just to let us know someone was there.

Chance and I reined in and looked around to see who it was, but before we got a good look several other persons came sliding down the bank out of the tree branches, and before we knew it we were surrounded by four men on foot, armed with various models of rifles. They closed in on us without saying a word.

"Don't shoot," said Chance, for of course we had our hands well up in the air by this time. "We haven't got enough money on us to make it worth your while, boys."

"This crew looks like they'd plug a man for his shirt, even with the hole in it," said I.

But here a voice spoke up from behind us, which we recognized as the original hold-up voice: "Quit that foolishness. It's you we're after, Marty Regan, and you know why."

"Oh," said I, quite calm now as I looked round. "Why didn't you say so in the first place instead of going through all these theatricals?" For you see, I had just recognized in the speaker my cousin Lem, who I hadn't seen in about five years.

I put my hands down and got off my horse as he came up to meet me. "How are you, Lem? How's everybody back home?"

"About the same," said Lem, which I already knew, of course. Nobody ever changes where I come from. "It's took us a long while to track you down, Marty. We burglarized your ma's house six times tryin' to get hold of one of the letters you wrote her, so as to get your return *add*ress."

"That's where you went wrong," said I, "because I haven't been writing her any letters. How'd you find me at last?"

"A fellow told me he'd seen your brother in Missouri," said Lem, "which, since everybody knows he's in Boston, we knew it was you."

"Hey," interposed Chance from his horse, where he was still sitting with his hands up, sounding a little apprehensive. As well he might, for the three remaining hold-up men had made a kind of tripod out of their rifles, with Chance at the summit. "If you know these road-agents, Marty, call 'em off, will you?"

"Don't worry, Chance," said I, "they never hurt strangers. The kids have grown some," I added, looking around at the other bandits.

"Ain't they, though," said Lem with uncle-ish pride. He'd trained himself up a squad of nephews that operated like something between Mexican *rurales* and the Baker Street Irregulars. They were deceptive in appearance, though, since they looked like ordinary Arkansas farm boys.

Lem turned to me. "Well, let's get down to it, Marty. If you want to, you could save us the time and trouble and just hand it over peaceable."

"You think I'm fool enough to carry it on me?" said I with dignity. "And you sure know me better than to think I'd turn it over without at least arguing some."

"Oh, quit borrowin' time," said Lem. "I hope your friend here don't object to bein' tied up for a few minutes, in case he takes it into his head to go for help while we're occupied."

"What are they going to do to you, Marty?" said Chance in alarm. I suppose him not being acquainted with my relatives, they sounded rather bloodthirsty to him at first.

"Only a little game of hide-and-seek," said I. "I'm at your service, Lemuel. He won't mind too much so long as you don't take all day, only mind you don't cut off his circulation."

So one of the Irregulars incited Chance to dismount with the tip of a rifle in the small of his back, and they tied his wrists together, and he stood by and watched while Lem and I searched me. I took off my coat and hat and showed Lem that none of the linings had been ripped, and we turned all my pockets inside out, and I even sat down and took off my boots and offered to do the same by my socks, but Lem didn't take me up on that. While I was putting myself back together he stood by frowning and biting his thumb, and you could tell he wasn't satisfied. Suddenly he looked up at Chance and then strode over to him.

"What about him?" he asked, pointing a finger.

"Who?" I said, looking up from putting my boots back on. "Oh, that's Chance Stevens. Sorry I forgot to introduce you fellows properly."

Lem nodded as if his suspicions had been confirmed. "Pretty smart, Marty," he said, "but not smart enough to fool me. Did you really think I wouldn't guess you might have slipped something to him?"

"Oh, balderdash," said I. "I couldn't slip him an ace during a poker game without him asking out loud, 'What's this?' You're wasting your time, Lem."

"Son," said Lem to Chance, ignoring me, "ordinarily we don't bother anyone who's not a member of the family, but under the circumstances it looks as if we'll have to temporarily adopt you. We can't leave any stone unturned, if you'll forgive the allusion. Hope you don't mind."

"What the heck is this?" demanded Chance, understandably mystified. He was a high-spirited young fellow, and wasn't going to submit to indignities without making some noise about it. "Marty never gave me a thing in my life except advice I didn't ask for, and you sure don't want that. Do you mean to say you're going to let him search me, Marty?"

"Well, I didn't mean to say that if I didn't have to," said I, noncommittal, "but that's what he means to do."

"You just try it, mister," said Chance to Lem.

"Boys," says Lem in a tired kind of way, and the bandits crowded in a little closer.

Well, Chance put up a pretty stiff fight, but as

his hands were tied and there were three of them holding on to him, they got him down in the end and Lem went through all his pockets, then shook him by the shoulder until his teeth rattled, like he was expecting something to fall out. I saw Lem take a look at his boots, but he desisted. I suppose he caught a look in Chance's eye that said he'd get a kick in the teeth if he tried it.

You'd think a second failure would have mitigated Lem to some degree, but it was just the opposite. He swelled up like a thundercloud and resorted to desperate measures.

"Fetch the rig out here," he says to the youngest of the youngsters. "This is a case for a higher power to determine."

The kid immediately departed into the tree branches. And believe it or not, in a minute we heard a cracking and squeaking and rustling in there, and out of the thicket emerged a pair of brown mules, followed by an antiquated buckboard, all wreathed in incidental greenery from their sojourn in the wood. This rig somehow made it down the bank and the kid maneuvered it into the road. Three nags that looked older than the buckboard and wearing saddles to match, with their bridle-reins trailing, completed the outfit.

Lem ordered me and Chance to get up in the back of the rig. They didn't bother to untie Chance's hands, and I didn't venture to suggest it while Lem was in his present mood, so I had to help Chance up after me. Lem was leading our horses around to tie

them up behind the rig when he noticed the saddlebags, and immediately went all out for strike three. He
called the boys and they dumped out the contents on
the floorboards of the rig, and began going through
them right there in front of our feet. You can imagine
Chance was pretty miffed by this. He sat there grind-
ing his teeth and no doubt blaming me up hill and
down dale, while my relatives gravely turned our
clothes and things inside out. There were some of those
cattle-cultivating papers in with Chance's stuff, and
one of the boys made a point of reading them all the
way through, like maybe he'd find an important clue
in them. He couldn't make head or tail out of it, so he
showed them to Lem, who made a big show of reading
them too, frowning hard, but I happen to know he was
no honor student in his day and he probably skipped
all the words he couldn't pronounce.

It was while he was doing this that one of the
other boys picked up Chance's hat from where it had
fallen in the scuffle, and tried it on for size. Lem looked
up from the paper and began to scowl in earnest. He'd
climbed up into the buckboard for a better perspective
on the investigation. "Quit that!" he says. "You know
we've never appropriated nothin' that didn't belong to
a member of the family. Mind your manners," says he,
and from where he's sitting he takes a swipe at the
boy's head and sends the hat sailing into the air.

Well, I don't know if he thought it was a joke,
or target practice, or if it was just pure deviltry on his
part, but the other boy standing by whips up his rifle
and takes a snap shot that sends the hat spinning ten

yards straight up. Before Chance's mouth had dropped open all the way the boy who'd started all the trouble ups with his own gun and drills another set of holes through it as it's coming back down. And then the kid on the wagon seat hauled his firearm up to his shoulder and blasted away. It was one of those big old muzzle-loading affairs, almost as long as the kid himself, and it billowed out enough black smoke for a cannon and the recoil knocked the boy clean off the wagon seat and head over heels in the dust, while Chance's hat went sailing off over the river like a bird going south for the winter. What's more, the four brown ears of the two brown mules zinged straight up like they were charged with electricity, and their eight hoofs went off like a thirteen-gun salute. The buckboard gave a jerk that threw Chance and Lem and me all in a pile on the floor, and those mules went tearing off down the road like they were trying to win a quarter-mile sprint.

CHAPTER FIVE

Dinner With Lem

THAT WAS a ride. I repeat, that was quite a ride, even though it only lasted ten or fifteen seconds. As soon as he realized what was happening, Lem began bellowing "Bail out! Bail out! Man overboard!" and he grabbed Chance and shoved him over the starboard side of the rig! In spite of being jounced around like corn in a popper, I still had a grip on my faculties, and I knew I'd rather jump to my death than be pushed to it. So I evaded Lem, scrambled to the back of the buckboard, took a big breath like you do before jumping in the water and launched. Next thing I knew I was making a kind of eggbeater of myself coming to a rolling stop in the road—and when I'd tumbled to my feet and turned round the other way a few times to get rid of the dizziness and stopped to take a look about me, the buckboard was gone!

It had vanished clean off the face of the earth. I stood stunned for a second, staring down the flat road to the curve of the river—then I realized what must have happened, and I started running toward it. Part of the way there I met Lem climbing out of a bush, which wasn't at all where he'd been aiming for when he bailed out, but which made as good a landing-place as any. We rushed up to the edge of the bank and looked over.

It was pretty much as I'd guessed. Instead of taking the curve in the road, those mountain-bred mules had rushed straight over the steep bank and down to the edge of the river—and when they got there, finding a few inches of sparkling shallow water to be the most frightening thing they'd faced yet, I suppose, they'd swung sharp left and turned the buckboard over on its side right at low-water mark. There they stood, still in harness, waiting for somebody to come right the rig and tell them to go on.

After I'd seen all this in a glance I tore back up the road to look for Chance, who I'd given up for dead. But I found him just getting to the top of the bank at the spot where Lem had thrown him overboard. By some miracle he wasn't hurt, just bruised and banged and had collected half the sand of the riverbank on his clothes, which shows the fellow who made that remark about rolling stones had no idea what he was talking about. He was madder than a hornet, too, and convinced that Lem had tried to manslaughter him. Because of this I didn't untie him, fearing he might try to return the compliment, but grabbed hold of his arm and led him down to the scene of the crash with the boys coming calmly behind us bringing the horses.

When we got there Lem was just kind of puttering around the buckboard observing how deep the side of it was buried in the sand, already quite a different fellow from the one who'd been yelling his head off a few minutes before.

"Doggone that boy," I heard him say to himself, kind of melancholy. "If I've told him once I told him a thousand times not to use a double charge onless he's huntin' bear."

When we'd turned the rig upright, all of us heaving at it, we discovered that every blessed one of our things that had been in back had got pitched clear into the water when the buckboard went over. I guess the current must have been stronger there than it looked, because there wasn't so much as a pair of socks in sight. You can bet this made both Chance and me pretty sore, but we didn't get a shot at protesting because Lem had taken charge of the situation again. The first thing he did was order the boys to tie me up too. I guess he estimated that my toleration of family eccentricities was wearing a little thin, and expected trouble from me in the near future. The two of us were loaded into the rig the same way we'd been before the fireworks went off. Lem got up on the seat; the youngest boy, his face all black with powder-burn, handed the lines up to him, and off we went, with the boys falling in behind us mounted on their broomtails.

Chance wanted to know, of course, where they were taking us and what they were going to do with us.

"Don't bother asking," I told him. "They don't

like spoiling surprises with a lot of hints. We'll find out soon enough."

He was going to say a lot more, probably on conventional subjects such as the scientific rancher waiting for us and all the time we were wasting, but he saw that he wasn't going to get any more information out of me than he was from my cousins, so he subsided and settled down to grind his teeth some more.

We left the road pretty soon and it was cross-country for the rest of the day, under trees and over hills that would have been frightening if I hadn't already seen what those mules could do. Towards evening as the sun was going down, we struck into a thick piece of woods and spent a while ducking our heads until we came out into a clear space ringed round with sizeable trees. Lem indicated that we would camp here for the night. And his first thought upon dismounting from the buckboard was for us. Wasn't that nice of him?

"Make our guests comfortable, boys," says he.

Lem's idea of making us comfortable was standing us up with our backs to one of the trees and winding twenty feet of rope around us. It wasn't exactly *un*comfortable, just rather limiting. But we had a first-class view of the whole camp, and having nothing else to do we stood there and watched while Lem and the boys took their time about unhitching and unsaddling and building a fire. It was an education in itself watching Lem strike matches one after the other without losing patience when they didn't catch.

I'm not after starting any more trouble in the

family by caricaturing my cousins, so you'll have to be content with a thumbnail sketch. To state it simply, Lem was older than me, bigger than me and balder than me, and we didn't resemble each other in the slightest. The boys were somewhere between their teens and twenties, all thin as fence-rails and about as talkative, and the two younger ones were brothers. I was never quite sure if they were twins or not, but I wouldn't have been able to tell them apart if one hadn't been short and the other tall.

By and by the whole gang gathers around the fire, and by the smell that presently issued forth it was plain they were making hash of the proverb about too many cooks. Chance and I began to melt, slowly, as far as the ropes would let us, for we hadn't eaten in hours and the scent of that stew would have driven a vegetarian to carnivorism. The cousins all settled down in relaxing positions and took their time about eating it, while we watched hungrily from the shadows.

Presently Lem came over to our tree with his plate in his hand, not deliberately to tantalize us, but because he's always been one who can handle business and pleasure at once.

"You've been awful quiet," he remarked. "I thought maybe you'd have seen the error of your ways by now, Marty."

"Look here," said I, bursting with indignation and starvation, "you did a better job of searching us than an experienced train robber, and came up with nothing. Do you really think starving us at the stake is going to make it magically appear?"

"It's not steak, it's stew," said Lem with his mouth full.

"A whole Thanksgiving dinner isn't going to conjure it up, Cousin Lem."

"What the heck are you talking about?" Chance put in.

"Oh, shut up," said I, and that startled him enough that I got a few minutes free of his interruptions to palaver with Lem. "If you're planning on using us as hostages, we'll be worth a lot less if we're diminished by starvation. And our brains will be muddled so we can't give you any valuable information, either."

"Well, I don't know," said Lem, considering his empty plate. "I've always heard the way to a man's heart is through his stomach, but I don't know where the path to his brain lies. However, I'm not unhuman, Marty, so I'll see what I can scratch up for you."

He went off to the fire, leaving me panting with gratitude and anticipation. Chance cut in again, a bit sourly.

"I don't know if it's occurred to you yet that I don't appreciate being dragged into this, Marty," he says. "And I don't have a clue what it's all about, so I can't even argue with them."

"Well, maybe that's why I'm not telling you," said I, perked up by the near approach of nourishment.

"You know it's not fair," protested Chance, who was somewhat unwound by the effects of hunger himself. He sounded like he would have been inclined to sniff if he were a few years younger. "If I'm going to be searched and pounded and hog-tied and starved for no fault of my own, I ought to at least know whose fault it is."

"We haven't quite determined that ourselves yet," said I. "Some say it was Cousin Lucinda's husband, others back Uncle Joe, and some hold that Grandma started it all. I incline towards the last view myself."

"What were those hoodlums looking for this afternoon?" said Chance, direct and to the point.

"It's a long story," said I, in a slightly friendlier tone. The classification of my cousins as hoodlums secretly gratified and amused me.

"I'd like to hear it," said Chance. He sounded rather sarcastic, so I gave in with a double motive, of satisfying his curiosity and punishing him by making him listen to a tale that is somewhat difficult to follow even when you have an inside view, like I do. I scrunched down against the tree trunk, settled myself more comfortably against the ropes, and related in so many words the circumstances I am about to describe in the next chapter.

CHAPTER SIX

What Grandma Started

YOU WOULDN'T think it to look at me, but my grandmother was a beauty in her day. A lot of young men covered a lot of miles of Arkansas countryside to come and camp out around her pa's farmhouse and glower at each other, and shove each other's elbows for first crack at offering to escort her home from church and out to dances. There was a pair of brothers in particular who were most eager in their attentions to her, and they pulled ahead of the field coming down the homestretch, though still neck-and-neck themselves. The older one mortgaged half his farm to buy a real fine ring for the wedding, for he was sure he had the edge. His younger brother can't afford to do this, so he thinks a little and decides to employ the Sporting Instinct. He offers his brother a span of mules against that ring that Grandma likes him best. The Brother of the Ring is confident of his preponderance, and allows he'll take him on. Younger

Brother goes around to Grandma and asks her if she'll have him, and the long and the short of it is she will. So he wins his bet, and the ring, and Grandma, and he uses the ring to marry her with and becomes my Grandpa. Older Brother, far from holding a grudge, becomes a bachelor and a hermit.

Well, time passes on, and after fifteen or twenty years of matrimony and five children Grandpa passes on. And a short time after that, doesn't the Bachelor Brother trim his whiskers and recommence courting where he left off. There were some who speculated over whether he had it in mind to make up his losses on the bet, or just to do the duty of a brother like in the Bible, or if he really did have a strong fancy for Grandma. He did become a hermit for her sake after all, even though he was still known as one of the most sociable fellows in the county. Anyway, after a decent interval he and Grandma become friendly again, and he becomes Grandpa II. And as they're frugal folk they use the same ring over again at the wedding.

Are you following me so far?

So the years go on again, and eventually Grandma becomes a widow again, and even more eventually, after a long and full life, she passes away at a good old age and leaves her family to divide up her estate. And that's when the trouble starts (doesn't it always?). For you see, during her second marriage Grandma had accumulated five more children. During her lifetime the ten had always got on well, but now, after half a century of amicable living, the rock on which they split was a green one—the little thing sparkling in Grandma's wedding-ring. Along about the time when everything else in the estate had been divided without much bloodshed, somebody politely wondered aloud who ought to have that ring, and the war was on.

The offsprings of Grandpas I and II both laid claim to the ring, and both sets put forward lots of good legal reasons why they should inherit. The first set thought they had the better right because they were the oldest *children*. The second set countered by saying that their father had been the oldest *brother*. The first ones said because their parent had used it to marry Grandma *first*—the seconds said because theirs had *owned* it first. And so on, and so on.

What complicated matters was the amount of time that had passed by now. The first set of children were verging on elderly and the seconds were middle-aged, so they all had plenty of grown children and the grandchildren were multiplying all the time, which swelled the chorus on both sides. Then there was the whole annex that had married into the family, who all had opinions of their own—mainly that the member *they* had affianced should come out the winner, honest claim or no.

Some of my relatives used to waste a lot of time moaning over how they wished Grandma had just made a will leaving it to someone specific, but what they really meant was a will leaving it to *them* specific. I wish she'd had the foresight to have it buried with her and saved everybody the trouble. But I suppose not even Grandma, who was a wise and foreseeing woman at that, could have foreseen the way her kith and kin would behave over that doggoned piece of jewelry.

Well, if you've ever been to a family meeting where everybody talks at once and nothing gets settled, take that and multiply it by about sixty-five and you'll have a pretty good idea of what the next few decades sounded like. Arguing over the ring got to be such a common pastime that the younguns just growing up, who couldn't remember Grandma very well, used to think feuding was something all grown-ups did for amusement. And then there were all the little sub-feuds within the two sets over which person would actually get to keep the thing in their jewel-box once the main question was settled.

But things really warmed up when a certain person took it into his head that he was going to end the whole feud single-handed. He was a bright young man who'd married one of Grandpa II's granddaughters, another half-step-third-cousin of mine. He was a lawyer, and he went and drew up a lot of papers claiming that Grandpa the First had never really owned the ring at all, because his bet with his brother was fraudulent and not recognized by Arkansas law, and therefore everything that had happened since was null and void. And he went and gave those papers to the circuit judge.

Well, when this got out, half the women in the First Set of the family had hysterics. None of my family had ever gone in much for law, and they took the bright young man's fancy language to mean a lot of accusations and implications he'd never dreamed of. One of my aunts got it into her head that he was saying Grandma hadn't been properly married at all, and what the younguns listening from under the dining-room table made out of this was that none of us really existed in consequence. But before any of them had a chance to try and figure *that* out, the menfolk finally agreed on something at a family meeting and went home and oiled up their flintlocks. You see, a feud in the privacy of the home is one thing, but having the family name read out in court was another. We could fling capital charges around by the handfuls on our own front porches, but putting them into a witness-box and the newspapers was anathema.

So a deputation of armed uncles called on the circuit judge, confiscated the bright young man's papers and scared the county clerk half to death. The way they saw it, the Second Set had broken all the rules of polite feuding and no holds were barred from then on. The old homestead became the scene of guerrilla warfare unmatched since the time of Francis Marion and John Mosby. Fourteen times that ring changed hands, and we lost count of the failed attempts at pilfering it. But strange to say, during all this time we kept on behaving as friendly as possible about everything not connected to items made of gold and green stones. As a fellow named Dickens once remarked, Union is Strength and Family Affection is Pleasant to Contemplate, and that might as well have been our motto. None of these we-aren't-speaking poses for us. Uncles and cousins might show up at each other's barn dances with black eyes and arms in slings from last night's campaigning, but that didn't stop everybody from having a good time.

I was one of the black sheep of the family, having dodged the draft into the family militia and left home to seek my fortune and a little peace. I went home a few years before the beginning of this story to visit my mother and see how the War Between the Sets was coming along. Ma was a little grey-haired lady who could be militant with the best of them, but she was a gentle soul at heart and she was getting tired of being woken up by the sound of scraps under her window every night.

"I've been thinking, Marty," she said to me, "that it would be good for all of us if we could take a little rest from feuding for a while. Not that I've changed my mind about who should have Grandma's ring, of course"—she sounded like she was trying to assure me she hadn't turned from Baptist to Presbyterian—"but I think the rest would benefit everybody. Poor Lucinda's health has never been good since your Uncle Tom tried to come down the chimney that night." (Lucinda was my cousin who had married the bright young lawyer.) "And your Uncle Jeffrey *will* persist in going scouting along Rush Creek at night with his boys, even though it always brings on an attack of his rheumatism tramping through the swamp. He isn't as young as he was, you know. No, Marty, I think"—she came up close to me and lowered her voice—"I'm sure my way is the best way."

"You've got something planned?" I said.

"I have the ring here," she said in an even lower voice, like she suspected there might be an Uncle in the chimney or a cousin in the china-closet at that very moment. "Your Aunt Sue smuggled it over to me in a basket of walnuts last week. Everybody thinks it's still in her tea canister. I want you to take it with you when you leave next week."

"Who am I to smuggle it to?" I asked.

"Oh, no one! Just keep it safe with you. You're going a long ways away, and it will be a long time before anybody realizes you have it and still longer before they track you down. Just think of the months of peace you'd be giving us, Marty," and she clasped her hands with such a heartfelt look that I got a picture in my head at once of the old wheat field gleaming all golden and free from skirmishers.

Put that way, I couldn't very well refuse, so when I said goodbye to everybody and rode away from home I had something in my coat pocket that they'd all have been very glad to have themselves.

I didn't mind it so much at first. But after a while, the warm and fuzzy feeling I got from the idea that I was doing something grand and noble began to wear off faster than the shine was wearing off the ring in my pocket. It was something of a nuisance carrying it around with me, because since I'd promised to keep it safe I couldn't bring myself to leave it anywhere. It got to be such a bother, what with occasional frights at finding I'd left it in my other pair of trousers, and having to switch it to my heavy overcoat when the weather turned cold, that I began to share Ma's opinion heartily and more so. In fact, I thought it would be a good thing for the family if the blasted thing was gotten rid of for good and all, not just temporarily.

That's how matters stood when Meredith Fayett inherited her aunt's ranch.

CHAPTER SEVEN

Chance Learns a Little More About My Family

WHEN I HAD finished telling this story, Chance Stevens was still looking at me so blankly that I began to wonder if I had been mistaken about his level of intelligence after all.

"I don't get it," he said. "What happened to the ring in the end?"

"Why, you numbskull," I retorted, "I gave it to Miss Meredith, of course, to use at *your* wedding."

Chance was saved from going off like a rocket by the ropes that held him to the tree, and Lem's coming back just at that moment with the stew he'd promised us. From the amount of time he took in getting it, and the amount of stew we found in our plates, I'm sure he must have been having another plateful himself in the meantime. He untied us without even warning us not to make a break for it, knowing full well we never would with that stew to hold us, and then he drew off a few yards and watched us cunningly as we sat down on the ground to eat. I suppose he thought one of us might try to swallow the ring or something.

Hungry as he was, Chance didn't start eating right away, but sat there a minute with the plate in his hands, frowning over it. "This needs some thinking over," he said.

"It's not poisoned," I assured him. "There hasn't been a life lost in this quarrel yet. I think it's a record for Arkansas."

"No, you idiot, I mean the ring. I'm trying to think how I should explain to your cousins."

"Don't," I said between mouthfuls. "I tell you, I'm done with the thing. Miss Meredith's welcome to keep it. This is the end of the feud so far as I'm concerned."

"Now, listen, Marty," said Chance firmly. "I feel real sorry for you with your family troubles and all, but you shouldn't try to saddle other people with 'em. I'm going to tell your cousin I know where the ring is and that I can get it back for him."

"And let Grandpa II's family come off winner?" said I with a contrary return of the old feudal spirit.

"I'd give it to Grandpa III if he existed. You've dealt yourself out, Marty, so this is my show. The question is, just how to do it. We don't want these hoodlums bothering Merry."

"Bothering who?" I echoed.

"Meredith, of course. I'm not going to spill that she's got *it* so long as they've got *us*. They might take it into their heads to go capture it themselves."

"So what do you propose?" I murmured. It's fun sometimes to see a kid like that get himself all worked up with an idea, even when you know it isn't going to work.

"Do you think they'd turn me loose to go and get it for them, keeping you as a hostage to make sure I come back?"

"No."

"Well, then, what if you went and I let them keep me?"

"Possibly," said I, "but there's two reasons why possibly not. In the first place, we never completely trust anybody we're related to, and they wouldn't want to risk being stuck with you. In the second place, I won't do it."

"Marty!"

"I've played my lone hand," said I, "and my stomach is full of stew, and I wouldn't be surprised if the kids came up with something just as good for breakfast. I like being a prisoner. Sooner or later they'll realize that, and then they'll let me go."

"Well, I'm going to have a shot at convincing them to let me go and fetch it, anyway. I don't think they'll be unreasonable. You're just too much of a pessimist where your family's concerned."

I didn't bother telling him that I had collected thirty-odd years of reasons why I should be a pessimist where my family was concerned. He wouldn't have listened. I just settled back to watch what was shaping up to be Act III of the comedy that was being improvised as we went along.

Chance was playing his part, all right. "Oh, Lem," he called out in an easy, friendly voice that ought to have put a far dumber person than Lem on his guard at once. "Come over here a second. I've got something to tell you."

Lem came stumping over again. He was an obliging kidnapper.

"Marty's been telling me all about this feud business," said Chance, "and I think I can help you out. I know where your grandmother's ring is."

"Is that so?" said Lem, turning his head a little on one side.

"Dead on the level. Now, I've got a plan how I can get it back for you. If you'll let me—"

Lem held up his hand. "Begin at the beginnin'," says he. "Where and when did it part company with Cousin Marty?"

"Why, he gave it to a girl," Chance began.

"A *what*?" said Lem, like he was a Hatfield hearing I'd given it to a McCoy.

"She needed it in a hurry to pay off a marriage—I mean to get mortgaged," I said hastily. "I was just doing a lady a favor, that's all. Tell him about it, Chance."

"But to get back to what I was saying," said Chance, ignoring me, "if you'll let me go, and keep your Cousin Marty here for a hostage to see that I come back—'cause I'm sort of fond of him, after all, and wouldn't want to see him get damaged—I'll go and explain everything to her and bring the ring back here to you. What do you say?"

"Where do *you* come into all this?" said Lem curiously, peering at him closely in the firelight. "How are you acquainted with this lady Marty spoke of—so as to be able to explain things to her?"

"I happen to be—er—married to her," said Chance, clearing his throat and flushing up a bit. I was glad to see he had enough self-respect left to be embarrassed over *that* situation.

"Don't listen to him, Lem," said I. "He's just trying to save himself. He's making up outlandish stories. He won't come back if you let him go."

"Marty!" Chance shouted again. "You said you were out of this."

"And I'm trying to stay out," I told him, "by ways and means. If that ring comes back into the family, I'm dealt in again."

"You double-crossing sneak," said Chance.

"This is all mighty interestin'," said Lem, rubbing his chin, "but it only recommences my suspicions that it ain't a matter to be settled in the woods. Young feller, you're going to have your chance to argue with the proper authority."

And that was all he would say to either of us, though of course Chance pestered him with questions for a bit till he saw it was no good.

Under ordinary circumstances you couldn't have paid me to go on a trip with both Lem and Chance. When not engaged in feuding Lem was an easygoing kind of fellow and never saw the need to hurry. Chance, on the other hand, was always champing at the bit to be going somewhere or doing something, like a high-spirited horse that'll race himself around the corral when there's nobody else to race. Fellows like that are fine working partners when you want to get a job done on the double, but they're wearing companions on a long trip. I'd only expected to be on the road with Chance for about a week and a half all told, which was bearable, but it looked like our little business trip was shaping up to be a regular voyage of discovery. I had an idea that the longer we took, Chance and Lem would start grating on each other like a couple of gear wheels turning at different speeds. But as it turned out I needn't have worried.

I think it was our reminiscing that put a damper on Chance. To while away the time the next day in the buckboard, I asked Lem for some more elaborated tidings of the folks at home. You know, who'd run off to get married and whose rheumatism was bothering them the most, and how many new babies had been born, and which aunt had won the blue ribbon for rhubarb pie at the county fair and things like that. Lem answered matter-of-factly, at length, and in detail. You always appreciate your family most when you've been away from them for a while, so I enjoyed it.

And of course one thing led to another, as they always do, and before you knew it Lem and I had got started on a good old-fashioned do-you-remember session. Every once in a while when cousins foregather they drag out of mothballs all the memorable moments in the family history clocked in during their lifetime, and a few winners that've been passed on to them second-hand, and give them a good airing. Well, that was what we did, and Chance sat still as a mouse and listened with a kind of scared look on his face. I don't know if you've ever noticed it, but while the behavior of your family seems perfectly normal to you, it comes across as pretty half-baked to an outsider. You know, the little peccadilloes and traits that make you say, "Oh, that's only Myra's way," or "Nobody minds Jack." People are oddly narrow-minded that way. My family was just like any other large and unaccountable family, only maybe more so, but I can imagine how nutty some of those anecdotes must have sounded to Chance.

But then again, the crazier a thing sounds the more people want to hear about it. Eventually Chance got interested in spite of himself and began to loosen up a little bit. He even laughed in the right places. I think he'd been rather afraid of my cousins at first, even though they were mainly harmless except when things went off by accident, but he got past that. Lem and the boys were the kind of fellows who you can't help liking even when you think they're crazy. When you come to think of it, Chance was sort of the same way. I suppose that's why he and I were pals.

So we all got on pretty amicably together. After a little while Chance and I were given the benefit of the doubt and allowed to ride our horses, which was a distinct improvement over the floor of the buckboard. Lem's leisurely pace kept us on the road so long that I began to wonder privately if we weren't getting close to the Arkansas border. That worried me a little. I mean, Chance seemed to have assimilated himself pretty well with this batch of cousins, but I couldn't answer for the result if you dropped him down unexpectedly in the middle of the whole clan. And I didn't hanker after taking sides either way in a situation like that.

But one cloudy afternoon we rode into a little town that to an experienced eye was still plainly Missouri, and Lem brought the cavalcade to a halt outside a little frame house with a picket fence and a garden that had been abandoned halfway through planting season. We dismounted and went up the walk, and no doubt were seen to do so from the front window, because the front door opened as we got to the steps. And right then any enthusiasm I'd been getting up for this adventure dropped right down into my boots and made my feet want to walk in the other direction, because Aunt Bertha was standing in the doorway.

CHAPTER EIGHT

Aunt Bertha

YOU MAY wonder why I've never mentioned Aunt Bertha up till now. Well, she was the kind of person you feel you ought to speak of in a whisper when they're not around. To put it in a word, Aunt Bertha was Formidable. My father, who was unashamedly afraid of her, used to say it wasn't respectful to call her a battle-axe, but she was definitely in the genus of sharp implements. She was big enough to be Lem's mother, which she was, and she had a personality to match her size. When she kneaded bread you couldn't help feeling sorry for the dough. Lots of people used to edge around and get a table between them and Aunt Bertha before giving her a piece of bad news. There still persists in Arkansas a legend that, at the age of eighty-six, Aunt Bertha chased an I.R.S. tax collector around the barn and out to the road. Well, I can set the record straight—it's no legend, it's a solid fact.

She had her hands on her hips as we came up toward her, and the look in her eye as it fixed on me was like the one she wore when she was picking out a turkey for Thanksgiving. I tried to look meek and unappetizing.

Her greeting wasn't exactly effusive.

"What'd you bring him back here for?" she demanded, pointing at me. She looked over the rest of the group, including Chance. "Who's that? Speak up, Lem."

"I can explain everything, Aunt Bertha," I began very meekly, but she cut me off. "When I want your explanations I'll ask for 'em. What are you waiting for, Lem? Where is it?"

Lem (about whom, by the way, you'd have wondered why you were ever intimidated by him if you saw him in the company of his mother) was scratching his head and trying to think out how to do this without hazard to himself. "Well, Ma," said he, "to put it mildly, it's gone Out of the Family."

"What?" says Aunt Bertha, sharp, and we all jumped like nervous horses hearing a rattlesnake. I half expected to see her push up her sleeves and start for Lem slow, but she let him have just half a second and that's where Chance stepped in.

"Ma'am," he said, "what Lem means is that there's been a misunderstanding, and I'm sort of to blame for it. But it can all be fixed up if you'll just listen to the whole story. I'm sure you'll see what I mean."

I was purely grateful at that moment for Chance's way with womankind. He could be the next thing to charming when the occasion called for it, and if his manners didn't exactly melt Aunt Bertha's heart of stone, they made her go from homicidal to just plain grumpy.

"Well," she said grudgingly, looking him over with an expression that wasn't very flattering but had less of the executioner in it, "if you think you can talk sense you're welcome to try. Get in here, all of you."

We filed in and filled up that little box of a house. It was mostly front-parlor and antique furniture, and you could tell it was rented furnished by the pictures of somebody else's relatives along the walls. I marveled at the expense Aunt Bertha had gone to in her campaign to retrieve the ring. Lem, of course, was only a field-commander, and Aunt Bertha was the brain at headquarters that sent him hither and yon. She had moved her camp closer to the scene of the action because she always got impatient waiting for dispatches and Lem was none too good about sending them.

I never really stopped to reckon up how many different kinds of relations Lem and I were, considering that our mothers were first cousins as well as half-sisters. My mother was the youngest of Grandma's first crop of kids and Aunt Bertha was the oldest of the second crop. And as for placing those nephews of Lem's in relation to me on the family table of contents, the very idea made me giddy.

Anyway, we sat down, us four principal actors around the little round mahogany table and the boys on whatever other piece of furniture caught their fancy. Lem and I were careful to get on the opposite side of the table from Aunt Bertha, and Chance got crowded in between us. He wanted to start talking right away, but Aunt Bertha silenced him with a gesture that looked like a French Revolutionary giving the order to let fly with the guillotine. She pointed a finger at Lem and he began at the beginning. That is, he told her all about the hold-up and what came after it, slowly and conscientiously, watching her nervously all the while like a kid looking at the schoolmaster to see if he's getting the answer right. His statements were all accurate, but of course Aunt Bertha didn't get the gist of the tale any more than you would if you only read Chapters Four through Seven of this story.

So she gave Chance his chance. (I ought to rewrite that, oughtn't I.) He took his cue from Lem and started back where he himself first came into the story, on the day Meredith Fayett made her proposal. I'll give him the credit of saying that he told it pretty much as it happened, without embellishing or making it sound any more ridiculous than it already was.

By the time he finished the boys were starting to fall asleep, and Lem was sitting with his mouth open and a glazed look in his eyes like he was listening to someone read Shakespeare. Aunt Bertha had her elbows on the table and her frown hadn't lightened a bit, and her chin was jutting out sharp like it always did when she was mad or thinking hard. The thing is, you could never tell which it meant, so people always stepped carefully around her when she had on that look, just in case.

Of course Chance didn't give Aunt Bertha the exact reasons he'd given me for wanting to be the ring-bearer, but he did wind up his story with the polite proposition that he should start for home as soon as possible—alone—and bring it back for them.

Aunt Bertha slowly straightened up in her chair before answering, and all my cousins woke up suddenly.

"Well, I don't know," she said. "I've got to think this over good before I make up my mind. And I want to have a talk with Marty alone."

She put an awfully sinister significance on that last word, and accompanied it with a glare at me. I'd been able to avoid a personalized lecture from Aunt Bertha pretty much all my life, but I didn't see much hope of escaping it now. But I got an unexpected reprieve. Aunt Bertha stood up and smacked the palm of her hand on the table, and a couple of little china figurines in the middle of it toppled over. All the cousins snapped to attention again.

"Let's have supper," she said, and made it sound like an invitation to the dungeon.

We got that later, although it was overhead instead of underfoot. After supper, which was good, I'll admit, Aunt Bertha marched Chance and me upstairs like a wardress and condemned us to a spare room. It was about three-quarters of the space between two attic rafters, with a couple of beds crammed into it. Aunt Bertha shut the door with a bone-jarring crash and intoned a blood-chilling goodnight from the other side, and we were left alone.

I couldn't believe how cool Chance took it all. He had already sat down on one of the beds and begun pulling his boots off, humming to himself. He looked up and found me staring at him.

"What's the matter, Marty?" he asked. "You look like you've lost your best friend."

"My best friend has lost his mind," said I, sitting down on the other bed facing him. "At least that's what I assume, because if he had a mind he'd have sense enough to be scared."

Chance just laughed at me, like he'd done when I warned him against marrying Meredith. "Poor Marty," he said, "you've got your fearsome aunt blown all out of proportion. But I'm not afraid of her."

"Her proportions are big enough the way they are," I said gloomily as I began to get ready for bed. It was no use arguing with Chance. Some men simply have no common sense when it comes to women of any shape or size.

I woke up at about midnight. There was a little moonlight, not enough to see by, but I could tell Chance was asleep by the sound of his breathing. I got up and put my clothes on mostly inside-out in the dark, took my boots in one hand and tiptoed out of the room.

I thought I'd been pretty quiet, but before I took two steps toward the head of the stairs somebody clamped a hand over my mouth. I had a second of terror thinking it was Aunt Bertha before I remembered she couldn't have been behind me. The hallway was too narrow for her to have squeezed into the corner next to the door.

Chance walked me backwards into the room and shut the door quietly without letting go of me.

"All right, Marty," he said in a loud whisper, "what's all this?"

I made him understand that I couldn't answer until he took his hand off my mouth. He obliged, and I gave him a loudly whispered list of good reasons why I should be absent at roll call the next morning. The way I saw it, my responsibilities had ended when Chance began formal negotiations with Aunt Bertha, and I'd only cramp his style if I hung around. Furthermore, I made it plain I wasn't going to stay anywhere long enough to be the subject of a private conference with said Aunt for all the blood and water in the history of American feuds. I was going and going now, thank you very much, and so—

"Oh, no you're not," said Chance. "If you disappear you'll get your folks riled and throw a wrench into my plans. Don't forget, you got me into this and you're not running out on me till it's over."

"I'll throw a bigger wrench into your plans if I've got to pitch into you before you'll let me go," said I. "Aunt Bertha doesn't take kindly to people who make disturbances in her attic late at night. And let me remind you that if you hadn't gone against my advice and gotten yourself married you wouldn't be here at all."

"Are you going to start that all over again?" he demanded.

"If you don't let me make my exit without

fanfare—you bet."

He let out an exasperated sigh and let go of my collar, and sat down on one of the beds with a thump. I thought I'd won the argument and turned to go, but he was back up and buttonholed me again before I finished turning.

"Look here," said he, "maybe we can make a compromise."

"Compromises never work in Missouri," I said.

"You stick by me," said Chance, "and I'll see to it that your aunt doesn't get at you without a referee. I promise. I won't let her catch you alone. Deal?"

I thought it over. Maybe it was the safer course. Dodging Aunt Bertha on my own was only putting off the evil day for a time.

"All right," I said. "But if you come up short, I'm gone and you can find me in California, if you really want to see me that much."

Chance gave another sigh, of relief this time, and told me to go back to bed. He beat me to it and was asleep in five minutes.

The next time I woke up it was morning, and the first thing I saw by daylight was that Chance was gone.

I was mad. I knew what he was up to. He'd decided to slip out and go off on his own without waiting for official sanction. I was enraged, and beyond that I could have told him it was no use, for Lem & Co. would simply go after him and bring him back tied up in knots. I was angry. So that's why he'd been so anxious to keep me in last night! I was going to be the scapegoat. I was furious. I thought he'd woken up awful quickly when he was supposed to be sound asleep. "Double — double — double-crosser," I sputtered as I untangled myself from the quilt and scrabbled under the bed for my left boot. I dressed quicker than I ever had before and tumbled down the stairs, but almost at the bottom I heard a sound that stopped me in mid-tumble. It was the sound of laughter coming from the kitchen.

I burst in the kitchen door and skidded to a stop. Aunt Bertha was standing at the table abusing some eggs for breakfast, looking not just grimly pleased but like she was actually seeing the point of something funny. And leaning against the wall by the stove was Chance Stevens, looking not so much like an octuple-crosser as he looked like Aunt Bertha's best friend in the world, and not going anywhere in a hurry.

 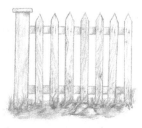

CHAPTER NINE

Family Meeting

WELL, IT WAS about this time that I began getting the feeling I'd gone from a prominent speaking role to a walk-on. Maybe even just a prop, for my primary function over the next few days was getting fallen over. It was a little house and my cousins didn't operate well in narrow hallways.

Chance Stevens acted like he'd been understudying the lead all his life. I guess Aunt Bertha had given him an encore, because he told her a whole lot more about Meredith, and the improvements they'd been making on the ranch, and about the neighbors and town and whatnot—leaving out all the names, of course, to protect the unsuspecting from a visitation by my cousins. Aunt Bertha laid all kinds of traps for him, but Chance side-stepped them all as neatly as if he'd been playing blind-man's buff with a hole in the blindfold. For the funny thing was, with all their friendliness it was plain to me that Chance didn't trust

Aunt Bertha or Lem any further than you could have thrown them, which wasn't far, let me tell you. He still had some first impressions stuck in his head that had a lot to do with rifles and sandbanks. I think he expected that as soon as he'd given them the coordinates of the ranch, he and maybe I would be tied up in a closet somewhere while Lem & Co. went kiting off to conduct another ambush on Meredith.

On the third day after our arrival I ran into Aunt Bertha in the hallway.

"Marty," she said, while I was recovering from being bounced off the wall, "I want you in the parlor. We're going to have a—where do you think you're going?"

"Under the terms of the Missouri Compromise of 1902," said I, "attendance isn't compulsory. I'm going to look for my bodyguard."

"Quit your nonsense," said my aunt. "We're going to have a family meeting—"

("Oh, no," I groaned.)

"—and I've asked Chance to take a walk out in the garden until we're finished."

I had to go to the window to reassure myself that it wasn't a decoy on Aunt Bertha's part with a sight of Chance walking up and down by the fence with his hands in his pockets, and looking like he had something up his sleeve too.

In the parlor all the cousins were sitting up straight and stiff and self-conscious. They weren't used to participating in official pow-wows. That was the department of Aunts and Uncles. I heard one of the boys ask Lem if we had to observe elementary procedure, and Lem said no, he didn't think so, just wait for Aunt Bertha to tell us when to talk. Being the only Aunt present, she had elected herself chief speaker and chief justice by default. If she'd ever been a real judge in a courtroom she'd have gotten nothing but convictions, because she would have scared the witnesses into admitting everything.

"The question is," began Aunt Bertha once she was seated at the table, bringing her hand down on it deliberately for emphasis, "what we're going to do."

It may have been a question, but she didn't ask it as one, so nobody answered.

Aunt Bertha looked hard all along the line of nephews to see if anybody was going to lodge an objection, and since you can guess what the answer was to *that* she passed on to the next order of business, which was answering the question herself.

"We are going to get the ring back," said she.

I said, "How are you going to —"

"Be quiet, Marty," said Aunt Bertha.

I thought to myself, if she says the next question is how are we going to get the ring back, I'm going to filibuster something.

One of the nephews looked like he wanted very much to say something but didn't dare. He tried looking noticeably uncomfortable, probably hoping Aunt Bertha would notice and tell him to speak up, but all he got was a sharp command to "stop that fidgeting." I had my elbow on the table and my chin resting in my hand, and I moved them as a precaution in case that might be classified as fidgeting, then changed my mind and put them back. I was in kind of a rebellious mood.

"Chance has offered to go and get it for us," Aunt Bertha went on. "The question is—"

"Is this a different question?" asked Lem.

"Don't interrupt," said Aunt Bertha so fiercely that Lem grew a few sizes smaller before my eyes.

"If the question is anything about Chance," I put in, "I can answer it. I've known him for sev—"

"Be quiet, Marty," said Aunt Bertha.

I hope you won't think any less of me when I tell you that's just what I did. You never knew my Aunt Bertha, that's all.

"Where was I?" she said, frowning.

Lem murmured, "The question..."

"Is whether or not we're going to let him go," finished Aunt Bertha as if it were all her own idea. "In other words, whether it would be—"

"Or not be," I couldn't help adding. "That is the question."

"Which question?" said poor Lem.

One of the boys observed, unpermitted, that if we didn't let him go, wouldn't we have to think up some other way to get it?

Aunt Bertha smacked the table with the flat of her hand, jolting my elbow, and I bit my tongue. "Can't the lot of you ever learn to behave yourselves?" she thundered, rocking to her feet, while we all shivered in the force of the blast. "This is supposed to be a decent, organized family meeting! We'll never get anything done if you all don't quit talking all at once so a body can't hear themself think!"

A frightened silence reigned for a minute, while Aunt Bertha, who seemed to have swelled to twice her usual size, fixed us with an angry, gleaming eye, blowing hard through her nose like an indignant horse.

I ventured timidly, "If I could just get a point of order in here somewhere—"

"I'll give the orders," said Aunt Bertha. "Sit down and be quiet."

"I am sitting down."

"Well, stay there."

She sat down herself with a thud that made the lace curtains in the windows tremble. The cousins dared to poke their heads up out of their collars again.

"After a lot of consideration," said Aunt Bertha slowly—and we all leaned forward in expectation—"I think we all agree that Marty had better step outside for a minute while we finish up the last of our business. Go on outside with Chance, Marty, and wait till we call you."

Lem and the boys, who apparently constituted

a silent majority, looked at me enviously. I was so amazed by my good luck that it didn't occur to me until I was halfway through the door that I was being kicked out, and by an unfairly large quorum of the Grandpa II contingent at that.

"Say, Aunt Bertha," I began, turning back, "it seems to me that—"

"Will you GO!" she roared, and the echoes chased me all the way down the hallway to the back door. As family meetings go, that one was a dud. We were just too easy for Aunt Bertha to lord it over. Put her in a room with that many Aunts and Uncles of her own stamp and you'd really have seen something—if you wanted to, which I'd advise against.

Chance was still walking up and down out in the so-called garden, humming to himself and grinning every once in a while in a provoking way.

"Meeting adjourned?" he said as I came up. "How'd it go?"

"Oh, terrific," I said. "We accomplished as much as a joint session of Congress the week before Christmas. I was voted off the floor as a mistrial, and I'm waiting for the verdict."

Chance laughed. "Don't worry. The worst they can pin on you is transporting smuggled goods. And I'll post bail for you in precious stones."

"You know," I said sourly, "I think Aunt Bertha already knew exactly what she was going to do before she called that meeting! She just likes bossing people around. I'm convinced that rigamarole I just went through was a song-and-dance staged for *her* benefit."

"Of course it was," said Chance lightly. "*I* knew that all along. She's going to let me go."

I gave him an unbelieving look. "*You* knew! What do you know about my Aunt Bertha? It's absolutely indecent that you're not even afraid of her, let alone claiming that you understand her!"

Chance laughed at me again. "You watch. In about ten minutes she's going to call us up to the house and solemnly inform us that the tribal council has put my request in the peace pipe and smoked it, and the big medicine told 'em it's the right cure. Otherwise meaning that Marty's Aunt Bertha nodded her head three times—or maybe just once; that's enough to make you boys jump—and ordered them to turn us loose on parole tomorrow morning. You watch and see if I'm right."

This speech left me speechless. I mean, it left me crowded so full of things I wanted to say to him that none of them could get out.

"I talked her round, that's all," Chance went on, reverting back to Aunt Bertha in that contentedly idiotic tone that he used whenever he talked about women, which made me want to smack him on behalf of the whole male race. "It wasn't hard at all. The trouble with you, Marty, is that you're just not diplomatic."

"I knew that before," I said gloomily. "If I was, maybe I could have talked you out of getting married in the first—"

"Oh, will you shut up?" said Chance.

And we didn't say anything more until Aunt

Bertha put her head out the back door and called us up to the house.

The irritating thing, of course, was that Chance turned out to be right.

CHAPTER TEN

We Give a Surprise, And Get One

TO UNDERSTAND what happened next you've got to take into account just how long we'd been away from home. It should have taken us less time getting back than it did coming out, but it didn't work that way. Just after we left Aunt Bertha's headquarters the area was hit by some pretty hard rains, and we had to go around the long way to avoid some flooded roads and valleys, not to mention stopping over a few times when the weather was really bad. And then just when we were getting back on track, Chance's horse threw a shoe out in the middle of nowhere, and we had to waste some more time finding a blacksmith and getting it put to rights. Altogether, with one thing and another, it was going on three months from the time we'd left the ranch when we came in sight of the familiar piece of road leading up the valley into Culver's Corners.

"You know, Chance," I said as we jogged our

horses towards town, "there's one thing you haven't been figuring on."

"What's that?"

"Something I *can* claim being an expert on, taking into account some history you know of. The natural reaction of a female at being parted from a piece of jewelry."

"Who? Meredith?" said Chance. "Oh, shucks, I'm not worrying about that. Merry's a good sport. She'll understand perfectly." He pushed back his hat, the new one he'd bought on our way back to replace the one which the boys had shot up.

"Well, I don't know," I said. "Before we left home, she looked to me to have gotten awful fond of the thing for its own sake, aside from the sentimental value."

"Sentimental—what are you talking about?" said Chance, looking perfectly bewildered.

Really, he was embarrassingly thick-headed in some respects.

I pulled a long face and reached over and put my hand on his shoulder. "Sonny boy, women tend to be sentimental over anything connected with matrimony, not the least of which is wedding-rings. Savvy?"

"Oh, I wish you'd quit over this marriage business," said Chance, sounding annoyed. "How many times have I got to tell you that it wasn't real? And anyway, Meredith wanted you to keep the ring in the first place, remember? Heck, we only used the darn thing because the Judge said we had to have one.

How's a body going to be sentimental over a thing like that?"

"That wedding was as real as a rigged election," I told him, "and one of these days you're going to find that out for yourself. And I can't promise you I won't say 'I told you so'."

"You just don't know Meredith like I do," said Chance. "I still say she'll be all right. She'll probably think the whole thing is a good joke."

I had to be content with "humph"-ing in answer to that, for there really wasn't any other answer I could make. It's always embarrassing to have a pretty girl think your relatives are a good joke, even when you think so yourself.

When we got about halfway down the main street I began to notice people looking at us a little oddly. Some of them were just plain staring, and after we'd passed by I heard the whispering sound that means people are pointing at your back. As we went by the general store on the corner Chance waved a hand to the storekeeper, who was standing on the steps, and he dropped his broom and bolted inside like he was running to tell his wife something. I hadn't thought people would be so glad to see us back—or sorry, because I couldn't tell which it was.

A little further along the street was the office of our old friend the Justice of the Peace. As we came abreast of it Chance said, "Say, let's stop in for a minute and say hello to the Judge while we're here."

I was agreeable, as I'd always found the old gent amusing, and we pulled up and dismounted.

The door to the office was standing open, as it was a warm day. When we got up to it and I looked in, there he was, plump and bald as ever, sitting at the desk fussing and frowning over some papers and refreshing himself every now and then from a glass of lemonade.

"Afternoon, Judge!" said Chance.

The J. of the P. and his chair jumped about a foot backwards together, clear to the wall. He got up, stumbling over the legs of the chair, staring at us and gasping, dabbing all over his face with a handkerchief and feeling himself around the heart to make sure it was still there.

"Good gracious me!" he gasped.

For once Chance and I were equally puzzled. We looked at each other, and then Chance said, half laughing, "Well, gee whiz, Judge, I know we've been on the road a long time, but I didn't think we looked that frightening."

The J. of the P. dropped down into his chair like a marionette when you let go of the strings, and went at it with the handkerchief again. "But you—you're—"

He broke off and squinted hard at us again, like maybe he thought his eyes were playing tricks on him and he was making a fool of himself by being scared of somebody else. But it was undoubtedly us, as either one of us could have told him if he'd only bothered to ask. He realized this and gave another combination gasp and groan. "But you two are supposed to be dead!"

"Why?" I asked.

"Don't be an idiot, Marty," said Chance, and then made himself look twice an idiot by repeating the question: "Why, Judge? What gave you that idea?"

"Why, the sheriff from Radley Hill," said the J. of the P.

It was logical enough once we got him to explain it. The scientific rancher near Radley Hill that we'd originally been going to see had been expecting us, and when he'd been going on expecting us for a week longer than he was supposed to, he decided to wire Meredith Fayett and find out if there'd been some mistake. She replied that we'd left home more than two weeks ago and hadn't been heard from since, and together she and the rancher came to the alarming conclusion that something must have happened to us on the way.

So the sheriff of Radley Hill went out to take a look round where we'd last been heard of. He couldn't pick up our trail beyond where Lem had taken over making it, but by pure chance his deputy found some of our things that had been pitched from the runaway buckboard washed up in a shallow elbow of the river —some clothes, and an empty pair of saddlebags. And they found Chance's hat that my cousins had been skeet-shooting with, with six bullet holes in it, through and through. That's how good they were with those old rifles. The sheriff, with a mighty long face, brought the stuff to Culver's Corners and showed it to Meredith, and she identified it as ours, all right. Putting this and that together, the sheriff figured we must have been killed by road-agents who'd stolen our horses, and that they'd dumped our bodies in the river along with the other stuff, which they must have turned inside out looking for money. The sheriff said it must have been a particularly vicious gang, judging by the amount of bullet holes in that hat. He didn't hold out much hope for ever finding hide or hair of Chance and me. They dragged the river in a few likely spots, but of course came up with nothing.

Knowing, of course, what had really happened, Chance and I couldn't help busting out laughing at the end of this tale, which the J. of the P. delivered in as mournful a tone as if he still thought we were dead — or was sorry we were alive. We laughed till we couldn't any more, and then Chance said, still trying to get his breath, "Well, it was nice of you all to be so concerned about us, Judge, but I guess we'll have to disappoint you. As you can see, we're very much alive — factually, literally and legally."

Instead of being pleased the old gent leaps up with another howl.

"Ooooh!" he yelped like a coyote that had got its tail stepped on. "This is simply terrible! How could it have happened?"

"Well, suffering sassafras!" said I. "I knew suicide was a crime, but what do they give you for resurrecting yourself?"

The Justice gestured helplessly. "It isn't that, it's Miss Fayett!"

"What about her?" said Chance, turning serious right away.

"She isn't to blame, of course, because she

couldn't have known—and it was only natural, being an attractive young woman, you know—but good gracious, what a dreadful predicament!—I'm sure I've never dealt with anything like this before—"

"What, what, what?" we chorused frantically.

The Justice of the Peace wrung his fat hands. "She's going to be married again!"

Chance turned an odd color I couldn't quite put a name to, and fell back a step like he'd suddenly lost his balance.

"Married!" he said, like he'd never heard the word before.

Right then, I smelled trouble. I didn't know what it was yet, but I saw it coming, plain as the nose on Cyrano's face. But the J. of the P., being the kind of person who can't see anything but his own troubles, worried on.

"Yes, yes! She told me just the other day. Oh, good gracious me," he intoned once more, with another application of the damp handkerchief.

"Who's she marrying this time?" I asked.

"Roger Torrance," said the J. of the P.

Chance sort of staggered again.

I had always liked Meredith fine, but my estimation of her dropped a good bit when I heard that. Roger Torrance! Oh, he combed his hair in the right direction and wiped his feet when he came in the house, if that's what she wanted; but I'd always figured Meredith had enough sense in her make-up to want a fellow with a little something behind the false front.

Considering the way Chance had been going on about her being such a fine girl and a good sport and all that not half an hour ago, I couldn't help thinking it must have been a little mortifying to him to find she was only another easy mark for a smooth-talking imposter like Torrance. I-told-you-so-ing is a bad habit of mine, even when I only think it. But when I looked at Chance to see if I'd told right, I had something of a jar, for it looked like something more serious than mortification had set in. His jaw was kind of hanging slack and there was a mournful sick-calf look about his eyes, and when you get those symptoms together it means just one thing.

The Justice of the Peace seemed to have wrung most of the energy out of himself with the sweat, and didn't have anything further to say except an occasional lugubrious reprise of his old refrain, "oh, good gracious me." He and Chance weren't going to be any comfort to each other, I could tell, so I batted the old gent on the shoulder and told him to cheer up, all was not lost, or something like that, and then I steered Chance outside and planted him near the edge of the porch with a post for support. Then I waited. Whoever said we haven't got any tact in our family?

Chance was quiet for longer than I'd ever known him to be of his own accord—about five minutes. He wandered off the porch and got the end of my horse's rein in his hands, and stood there turning it until it was twisted like the ribbons they hang at parties, clear up to the bit. Gradually he got to re-semble himself again, but himself in a very suspicious-looking mood.

"What now?" I asked, almost as meekly as if I'd been inquiring of Aunt Bertha.

"Home," said Chance darkly, and made that one word sound more forbidding than Aunt Bertha herself could have done...almost.

Chapter Eleven

Welcome Home

NOBODY SAW us ride in when we got to the ranch. All the hands were off somewhere and the yard was sunny and quiet. We dismounted by the porch and went up into the house—the door was standing open and we just walked in.

Meredith was in the front room and didn't hear us come into the house; she didn't even know it when we came to the doorway of the room. She was sitting at the desk writing something, in a patch of bright sunlight from the front window that lit up the red-gold of her hair. I noticed, though, that she looked maybe a little paler and thinner than she had the last time I saw her.

"Hello, Meredith," said Chance.

I don't suppose anybody had ever taught Chance the value of breaking things to people gently. Meredith looked up, startled, and saw Chance in the doorway. She leaped up, her eyes growing wide as saucers and her face getting even whiter than before, put her hand to her heart like she was finding it hard to breathe, and then gave a gasp like all the air going out of a balloon and tumbled down in a faint.

Chance had her up on the sofa before you could have said "Welcome home." And then he kind of stuck fast and started looking helpless and panicky, so I took off my hat and flapped it around Meredith's face until she started to come to. It didn't take long. In a minute or so she sighed and opened her eyes. The first thing they lit on was me, and I couldn't be mistaken for a ghost at close range, so I think that made her feel a little better. She sat up slowly, looking around until she found Chance, and that was the last anybody paid attention to me for the rest of the conversation.

Oh, I'm not complaining. Being a wallflower can be an interesting occupation, so long as you've got enough patience to keep from busting out with an opinion on all the idiotic behavior you witness while wallflowering. I might not be overburdened with patience, but I think I increased my stock somewhat during this adventure I'm telling you about. I had to.

But I'm wandering here. What I meant to say is, people will say and do a whole lot more interesting things in front of you than they would otherwise, if you're the kind of person who's easily overlooked.

But on this occasion it didn't look like anyone was going to rise to any memorable heights of oratory.

Meredith said, "Then—you're not dead?"

Chance said, "Well, no—I'm not," sounding as if he knew the obviousness of the answer. A lot more patiently than he'd have said it to *me*, though.

Meredith began to sniff shakily, as a girl will after getting over being scared, and to hunt around for a handkerchief or something to hide it. In my capacity as stagehand I fished one out and handed it to her, and she took it without thanking me. She disappeared behind it and made a few small sounds that sounded like she was buried under a featherbed, while Chance stood by uncomfortably trying to pretend he wasn't there. After Meredith had crumpled and uncrumpled the handkerchief a few times she regained her composition somewhat, cleared her throat and put on the unsteady dignity of a woman who's ashamed of having gone to pieces and is trying to pretend she didn't.

Chance said in a flat, clipped voice that was new to me, "I saw the Justice of the Peace on my way through town."

"Oh," said Meredith. From being white she turned an interesting shade of pink. "Then I—suppose he told you…"

"Yeah, he told me," said Chance. "Another business deal, I suppose?"

There was a sarcasm in his voice that made this wallflower's eyes pop open to a considerable degree. "Hullo!" said I to myself. "Good old Chance seems to have developed a respect for the sacred state of matrimony all of a sudden. Which wasn't at all present on another occasion I could name."

"Well, no," said Meredith, "I mean, not like that—exactly. It all happened rather quickly, you see.

We thought, of course—I mean I thought, and afterwards when Rog—that is—I never had any idea," she finished, managing one mostly complete thought at least. "If I'd known you were...I never would have thought of—"

"I'm sure," said Chance. Polite but short.

Meredith looked up at him appealingly. It struck me that she was sure making a lot of excuses, or trying to make them anyhow. What did she have to answer to him for? Under the terms of that little bargain they'd struck hands on it seemed logically unnecessary. Three months might have been a little hasty for a genuine grieving widow, but for a girl who'd been married to the back-payment on her mortgage I didn't think the usual rules would apply.

I suppose now that she had Chance in front of her for comparison, she was embarrassed at having to confess being linked up with a Roger Torrance on any terms. That reinstated some of my respect for her, because there's always hope for any girl that can still blush over that, and Meredith was doing a mighty fine job of blushing. And she was still mangling my handkerchief at the rate of a mile a minute, so that I began to entertain serious thoughts of asking for it back. Before I could do that she seemed to notice it in her hands for the first time and put it aside on the table beyond her.

"Well," said Chance—and I could have sworn he emitted something about as close a cousin to a sigh as Lem's nephews to me—"there's no point in getting upset. You remember what we agreed on before—"

He hung there until Meredith realized he was

waiting for her to say she did remember and nodded hurriedly, and then he went on, "So there shouldn't be any trouble. I'll be going back to town. I'll talk to the Judge, and I guess he can get you a—a divorce, or an annulment or whatever it was."

His face sort of twisted as he said it—Meredith wasn't looking at him just then—and all of a sudden I knew why she'd turned to Chance for help in the first place. He was a gentleman through and through, and I guess with some kind of woman's instinct she'd known she could trust him all the way. All at once I was feeling surprisingly ashamed of myself for coming down so hard on Chance lots of times before. All right, maybe he *was* a fool when it came to women, but you had to respect the way he treated them. You can't buy that kind of real deep-down old-fashioned chivalry, or whatever you want to call it. You know what I mean, don't you? Sometimes the words in the dictionary just don't cut it when you're trying to describe something like that. Little Meredith Fayett had no idea what a whale of a deal she'd really made that day in the J. of the P.'s office.

And then I remembered Roger Torrance and my liking for her went right down the thermometer again.

She nodded quietly in answer to Chance. I realized she was twisting Grandma's ring round and round her finger until it practically made me dizzy.

"I'll let you know what he says," said Chance uncomfortably, "and if you have to sign anything, or—anything."

She nodded again.

There was a pause, that became a long pause, and was just turning into a very long pause when something—a floorboard I think—creaked, and Chance got all severe again. I think he'd been waiting to see if Meredith would say anything, but she didn't, and young fellows like him have only a limited supply of optimism, not to mention patience. "I'll be going then," he said.

Meredith looked up quickly. "Thank you," she said in a soft voice. Anyone would have noticed how different it sounded than when she'd thanked him for marrying her, but the clock had struck midnight so far as Chance was concerned and he barely even nodded. He swung around and strode out of the house and I clumped after him, feeling more like a mouse disenchanted into a camp-follower than the other way around.

Chance didn't waste any time fooling around with reins this time, but grabbed them up short in a way his horse didn't exactly like and mounted. I looked at him more sympathetically than I'd ever have done if he'd been looking at me. For I'd been catching on, even if you haven't, and in case you haven't I'll spell it out for you. Though Chance had been laughing it off to everybody, including himself, it was plain to see he'd developed some genuine husbandly feelings for that girl, and was having a hard time coming to terms with the fact that he'd never be her husband—not really.

Even if I'd only half suspected this by the way

he acted around Meredith, I'd have known for certain by the way he behaved once we were out on the open road again. Chance wasn't one to sulk. He was pretty sensible about accepting his defeats once he got over having his initial fit. But this was a different Chance altogether. He'd taken longer than usual to rebound after the Judge's staggerer, and this time it didn't look like he was coming back at all.

I must have been a little preoccupied myself, thinking all this over, because I didn't notice we'd taken the wrong fork of the road until we were pretty far along it. I mentioned this to Chance. He didn't say anything, just swung his horse around and cut across a field instead of going back around by the road. Which was why we hit town a few blocks away from the J. of the P.'s office, which I supposed was what we were pushing for. But again, we never got there.

For you see, at just the right moment, or just the wrong moment depending on how you look at it, Chance looked up and discovered that we were coming opposite Roger Torrance's office. What's more, Roger Torrance himself was again standing on the porch.

Torrance must have already heard what had happened, because there wasn't the ghost of a chance that he thought Chance was a ghost. I never knew anybody yet who could look at a ghost that way, even in broad daylight.

Chance drew rein and looked straight back at him. I eyed them both a little anxiously.

"Hello, Chance," said Roger Torrance. "I

certainly didn't expect to see *you* back here."

"I guess not," said Chance.

His tone didn't invite further conversation, but Torrance laughed like neither of them had a care in the world. "Of course it really doesn't make any difference," he said, adjusting his tie (as if he had ever exerted himself enough to make it move out of place!). "Meredith told me all about your—arrangement. I must say it was awfully nice of you. Now that she doesn't need you any more, I'm sure you can get out of it to the satisfaction of everybody."

He tapped the brim of his hat a centimeter to the right. I imagine he was so used to doing it that he didn't need a mirror to measure. Oh, he was a decorative fixture all right. But I wasn't admiring him, I was watching Chance, who looked like Mount Vesuvius right about the time the Romans should have packed up and headed for the hills.

"Well, now, I don't know," he said, and I winced, because his voice was loud and had that sarcastic edge in it again, and something told me that edge meant trouble. "Maybe I'm tired of being nice and obliging. I've got my rights, haven't I? Meredith's still my wife after all. Maybe I'm not inclined to let her go! I sure as heck don't think much of her choice. With somebody else it might have been different—but you're *such* a rat, Torrance, I'm *sure* you understand."

Any other time that last line would have doubled me up with laughter, especially the way Chance said it, but I was too breathless with expecting disaster to waste any more breath laughing.

"Just what do you mean by that?" said Roger Torrance, his eyebrows wandering downward a little.

Chance, who was getting more reckless every minute and looking like he enjoyed it, wheeled his horse around and the horse entered into the spirit of the thing and reared. "You figure it out!" he shot back over his shoulder, and then struck spurs into his horse so savagely that it was all I could do to get mine underway before he was out of sight.

CHAPTER TWELVE

Some More Give and Take

NOW, I DIDN'T believe for one minute that Chance really meant what he said about not letting Meredith go. He wouldn't have done a thing like that to her for all the Torrances in the world. But I caught a glimpse of that particular Torrance's face as we left him in the dust, and he thought Chance was serious, all right. He hadn't known him long enough (as I had) to know the kid was just blowing off steam. You see how easy it is to get in trouble by taking somebody at their word.

I didn't catch up with Chance until we were well outside town, and then it was only because he slowed down some. "I thought we were going to see the Justice," I called out as I came up with him.

Chance consigned the J. to the wrong side of eternity and spurred his horse again so it pawed the air in the other direction.

"You said something once about starting for

California," he said.

"If you want to be rid of me, I don't have to go that far," said I. "Missouri's still big enough for both of us. But say," I added suddenly, "it won't be big enough to hold Aunt Bertha, let alone the three of us, if you don't deliver on the ring business. Why didn't you ask Meredith to give it to you while you were breaking up housekeeping back there?"

Chance sent the ring after the Justice without the slightest compunction. "You're a big help, Marty," he said, looking at me with such disgust that I had a feeling I might be next. It cheered me up mightily, because if Chance felt well enough to be mad at me he was all right. That fit of temper in front of Torrance's office had done him good. I thought perhaps he'd got back some perspective on how ridiculous the whole affair was.

"Where are we going?" I asked, for we were still moving along at a trot.

"California," said Chance crossly, which wasn't encouraging.

"I wouldn't advise it," said I. "We wouldn't be home in time for supper. And I'm hungry."

The best way to bring somebody out of a funk is to hit them square between the eyes with a good, hard, plain piece of practical common sense. Chance was silent for a minute, and then he gave a long, heavy sigh that said everything he hadn't put into words that day.

"Well," he said, "I guess—"

Right at that moment—I'm not kidding—we

came around a curve in the road, which was pretty thickly wooded just there, and came face to face with a buckboard and some saddle horses coming around it in the other direction. Only they weren't coming alone; they were inhabited by, namely, Aunt Bertha, Lem, and three nephews.

Did you ever have a dream where you're trying to get somewhere in a hurry, or do something very important, but every time you start out you keep being turned round the wrong corners and end up someplace else? You go through enough adventures to fill up the minutes of a semi-annual Knights of the Round Table meeting, but there's always something else you're supposed to be doing and you worry yourself into a case of nerves because the dream won't let you. And every so often you run against a completely non-sensical character who has nothing to do with the rest of the dream—say, a Southern Colonel carrying a freshly-painted ladder because he wants to climb into a birdhouse, or the disreputable fortune-hunter from the last novel you read, who's got a cold in his head and is hoping for an invitation to supper. Every time you go round the wrong corner, there they are coming around it in the other direction, with no purpose but to puzzle you and no better idea of what they're doing there than you have of why you're dreaming about them.

Well, that was the feeling I had. I believe that if Chance and I had started for California right then, I'd have expected to find behind every bush along the way an Aunt Bertha, and a Lem, and three nephews complete with buckboard, all looking exactly the same as when we saw them last.

Chance groaned, "Oh, for Pete's sake," and went slack in the saddle.

I wasn't half as upset as I ought to have been, considering that I normally regarded Aunt Bertha more in the light of my worst nightmare. I suppose I was just getting used to violent shocks.

Aunt Bertha was driving the buckboard, being a lifelong subscriber to the theory that you've got to do something yourself if you want it done right, and Lem was occupying the third of a seat left over and trying to look as if he liked it. We all drew rein when our horses' noses were within a foot of each other, and Aunt Bertha began nodding slowly like a malicious mandarin.

"Just as I thought," she said sourly. She elbowed Lem in the ribs. "I told you I didn't trust him worth a cent. Was I right?"

This smacked of being a rhetorical question, a thing Lem usually tried to avoid answering on the grounds that getting the wrong answer could be dangerous. So he just grinned at me uneasily, from which I gathered that I, and not Chance, was the untrustworthy party in question. It didn't surprise me.

Aunt Bertha pointed at Chance. "What's the matter with him?"

Chance had pulled his hat down low over his eyes, hoping, no doubt, that nobody would recognize him. I whacked him on the arm. "Wake up, Chance, we've got company."

He lifted his head and showed his teeth in the

sickliest-looking smile I ever saw. "De-lighted."

"Don't you be impertinent, young man," said Aunt Bertha, who was navigating her way down from the buckboard with Lem's help. She landed with a thud that I felt clear up through my horse's feet. "Get down here so I can talk to you—and so you can explain why you're on this road."

"Why, the woods are a little thick just here for traveling cross-country," said Chance sarcastically, dismounting. The sarcastic habit seemed to be growing on him—I suppose he'd picked it up from me. I didn't like it so much on him.

"It's not the road to Arkansas," said Aunt Bertha.

"No," I said, joining them on terra firma, "it's the road to California, or so I've been told."

"What difference does it make?" said Chance.

"You've broken your agreement, that's what difference it makes. Why else would you be going in *this* direction when you ought to be going in *that* one?"

"If we'd known what we were heading into we *would* be going in that one, let me tell you," said I.

"Be quiet, Marty," said Aunt Bertha.

"He will not be quiet," said Chance just as I opened my mouth to say the same thing. "He won't be quiet and neither will I. It's still a free country, isn't it? And you've got a nerve, I'll say, trailing us like this after you'd agreed to let me have a free hand."

"Trailin' you!" said Lem contemptuously. "We were two days ahead of you most of the time. Ma suspected Marty might put you up to something like this.

Now hand it over, Chance."

"I'll handle this," said Aunt Bertha authoritatively. "Now hand it over, Chance."

"I haven't got it," said Chance, folding his arms and looking stubborn.

"I don't believe you. Where is it?"

"It's on track to do duty at a fourth wedding," I told her. "You ought to be proud of it, Aunt Bertha. Not many rings can boast a career like that."

"Wha-at?" said Aunt Bertha, turning slowly toward me in a way that meant something.

"Chance," I said hastily, "you explain this. You're a good hand at explaining."

"No!" he said, and if he didn't stamp his foot he came close to it.

"He's going to be difficult," I told my assembled relatives, "and that's what explaining would be for me, so—couldn't you just be satisfied with my saying it's a long story?"

"No!" said Aunt Bertha, and her version was convincing. I took her aside, though still within striking distance in case I needed to call for help, and gave her a synopsis of the marital mess with Meredith, while Chance stood a ways off biting his lip and trying not to hear. Aunt Bertha listened, and frowned, and although I tried to make it clear to her that none of it was *my* fault, I don't think she believed me.

"You haven't made a particle of sense," she said when I'd finished. "I'd say go back to the beginning and try again if I didn't know it would be an utter waste of time."

"Thank you," I said.

You never saw three more mystified faces, by the way, than the ones on my half-step-second cousins all the time this was going on, and as for Lem, he'd long since given up trying to understand and gone round to the other side of the buckboard to get a little fresh air into his brain. Chance was looking as grim and unapproachable as it's possible for a nice-looking young fellow to look, but of course that didn't stop Aunt Bertha from approaching him. Confronting him would be a better word. She planted her feet apart and her hands on her hips and thrust out her lower jaw at him. "All I'm certain of is that *our* agreement had nothing to do with marrying or giving in marriage, and *you* are trying to back out of it."

"Oh, it was a bum deal all the way," said Chance, waving it away with his hand. "I was roped into this against my will in the first place; why should I be responsible? Marty gave it away; why not pick on him? Why pick on me?"

"Now you sound like Cousin Lucinda's husband!" I burst out. "Trying to crawl out of loopholes, are you? Well, let me tell you, Chance Stevens, I had as much right to give that ring away as anybody else in my family—which isn't much, I'll grant you, but—I've got my own good name to watch out for, and I'm not hankering after getting a reputation for giving in goodwill and taking back at gunpoint!"

"Will you mind your own business?" flared Chance.

"Oh, shut up!" I snapped back.

"SILENCE!" thundered Aunt Bertha.

When the oak trees overhead had quit reverberating, I tested an eardrum with my finger to make sure it was still working. Chance and Aunt Bertha were still glaring at each other in what had all the earmarks of being a stalemate. There wasn't a cousin in sight.

"Look here," I ventured mildly, "let's call an intermission of hostilities and count tens for a while, shall we? The darkest hour is just before—sunset," I added with a critical glance at the sky, "and besides which, I'm hungry. I'm sure things will look much brighter when we've got something solid in our stomachs."

Lem suddenly reappeared from somewhere at the word 'hungry.'

Aunt Bertha ruminated, and gave the hard sniff that came close to being a snort that she always did when she was trying to make up her mind. But food was a strong point with her too—another thing that runs in my family.

"All right," she said at last, speaking to me, I suppose, but keeping her eyes on Chance like she thought he might evaporate treacherously if she took them off him. "I could use something to eat myself. We've been traveling straight through and I'm worn to a frazzle."

Chapter Thirteen

Silver Tongue and Lead Bullet

WHILE THE pretty sizeable frazzle that was left of Aunt Bertha was bossing camp setup, Chance paced restlessly up and down by himself away under the trees. This was according to Hoyle for a fellow in his condition, so I let him be. But when the cousins had supper almost ready, I decided it was time to interfere. The pining-away part always struck me as unnatural. I mean, a man's got to eat.

"Come on and get some grub, Chance," I called out.

Chance shook his head without looking up.

"Leave him alone," said Aunt Bertha unexpectedly. "Sit down and eat, Marty."

I did just that. It was just what I would have suggested myself, and anyway, there was a mess of pottage stewing over the fire that was worth worse things than sharing it with Aunt Bertha.

As I told you before, none of my cousins were

big talkers, and my mouth was full most of the time, so there wasn't a sound except spoons going until we were almost finished. As Lem turned the stewpot upside-down to empty the last drops into his plate, I looked over at Chance and shook my head. I'd heard tell of such things, but I never believed until I saw it with my own eyes that a man could turn down that kind of dinner even for a bad case of unrequited love.

"Something's got to be done about this, Marty," said Aunt Bertha.

"It's too late for that. There's none left," said I.

"Not the stew, you idiot. Can't you ever talk seriously?"

"When I do, nobody listens to me," I said.

"Well, you'd better take care or people will start *taking* you seriously no matter what you say. They won't believe you've got the brains to invent that much nonsense on your own."

This awful threat silenced me for a few seconds, mainly because I couldn't think of anything to say, but it didn't hurt my appetite. Marty Regan is made of tougher stuff than that.

"For instance," Aunt Bertha went on so mildly that I knew she was up to something, "a while back you just as good as admitted that you were the one responsible for this whole mess."

I swallowed what I think was a small onion whole. "What!"

"You said you had a right to give it away to this Meredith girl, which, if that's not admitting you're responsible, I don't know what is."

"I'm *not* responsible for Meredith Fayett's acquiring more husbands and fiancés than she knows what to do with," said I, "or for Chance's taking a stubborn fit and refusing to get it back. And for Pete's sake quit euphemizing the thing. I believe in calling a ring a ring."

"Habit," said Lem with his mouth full. "Back home we never know who might be listening."

"As if anybody really thought you knew how to talk about anything else," I said scathingly. "But listen, Aunt Bertha, you haven't got anything to worry about. There's time. Miss Meredith can't get married again so long as Chance is alive and legal. As I understood it, he's got to absent himself—or was it vacate himself?— from the ranch for a year or so in order to nullify his end of the deal. Either that or commit a felony, and that's a little risky."

"We can't wait that long," said Lem, sounding alarmed. "Our grub's running low already. And I don't think the folks'll send us any more money if we don't—"

Aunt Bertha looked at him, and he got very busy trying to make the most of two drops of coffee left in the bottom of his cup.

"There's no question of waiting," said Aunt Bertha. "I'm warning you, Marty, that if you can't make Chance listen to reason soon I'll have to take drastic steps."

"You leave Miss Meredith out of it," I said instantly. "Otherwise I can't answer for your getting back to Arkansas in one piece, even if you are a lady.

Chance won't stand for it."

"Then go talk to him," said Aunt Bertha.

"You just got through saying that I was no good at that sort of thing. Make up your mind, will you?"

"You could be with half an effort. The trouble with you, Marty, is that you're just not—"

"Diplomatic," I said gloomily. "I know. But I can't help it. Some people are born with a silver spoon in their hand, and others with a silver tongue in their mouth. *I* inherited plain speaking along with a taste for onions and a family feud. Maybe that's why the feud's been running this long," I added, diverted for a second by the thought. "Doesn't reflect any too well on *your* diplomacy, Aunt Bertha."

She only grunted in reply.

I waited. She waited. Lem waited, and the boys, having nothing else to do at the moment, also waited.

"Oh, all right," I said finally. "I'll have a crack at it, but I'm not making any promises. Right now I'd be willing to trade in my spoon for the tongue habit—temporarily," I added, scraping the bottom of my plate.

When I was sure I had got every last bit of gravy, I put down my plate, got up and went over to Chance.

"Marty, do you know what I am?" was how he greeted me when I got near him.

I considered several possible answers, but none of them seemed likely to go over well, so I compromised with the usually-safe query, "What?"

"A fool. A doggoned, dad-blamed fool."

Since he'd just about plagiarized the essence of the speech I'd been about to make in a much more silvery manner, I couldn't do much more than spread my hands apart and shrug. If I'd been more diplomatic I probably would have said "Indeed?"

"How come you never realize these things till it's too late?" said Chance. He sat down on a log and pulled his hat way down over his ears. I felt sorry for him in spite of myself.

"You've got it pretty bad over that little girl, haven't you," I said.

"I didn't realize it until today," groaned Chance. "I mean, I always thought she was—and I used to think about her a lot when—but I didn't know I was…and then when the judge told me she was going to marry somebody else—it just hit me like a ton of bricks. And now it's too late—too late!" He pulled the hat down further so all I could see was the end of his nose.

I was wondering vaguely where I'd heard somebody talk in unfinished sentences before. It had a familiar ring to it, if you'll forgive the expression.

"Do you suppose," I suggested, more to make conversation than anything else, "that if you told Miss Meredith how you feel—"

"It's no use," came bleakly from under the hat. "She doesn't care a pin for me. Not that way. She'd just be *nice* to me—and try not to act surprised—and thank me for being her *friend*—and then go off and marry *Roger Torrance*—and I can't bear it!" Chance yanked his hat off and flung it on the ground with a fine gesture of despair.

I decided it was time to take matters in hand. All this emotion couldn't be good for his health. Besides, his new hat would be completely ruined if this kept up.

"Chance, you've got to get Grandma's ring back," I said firmly.

He bounced up and swung to face me. "I won't! I tell you, I'm not going near that place again. I want to forget all about it. I don't want to see her or hear her voice ever again. I couldn't face her and have her give me back the ring we used to—to—"

"Oho, who's taken up with the sentimental value now?" I said mercilessly.

"Marty, haven't you got any heart at all?" he said piteously.

"Of course I have. But mine's all in one piece, sonny boy. That's about as far as my knowledge of anatomy goes. Right now I'm trying to talk you into using your head, if you haven't lost that too."

"Use my head? At a time like this? My *head*?" sputtered Chance, as if he'd been some blue-blooded aristocrat being told to use his hands.

"Yes, your *head*, before somebody gets sick of your melodramatics and knocks it off for you!"

I'm sure Chance would have had an answer to that if just then somebody else hadn't joined in the conversation. A rifle spoke from somewhere in the brush—in a very unfriendly tone of voice, I might add —and Chance tumbled over at my feet.

Lem and the boys rose in a body and sailed out

of that camp like birds in flight. Aunt Bertha couldn't move that fast, but she just about burst a blood-vessel heaving herself to her feet and yelling after them to catch that no-good what's-his-name and bring him back here.

By the time she reached me I'd got my wits back. I turned Chance over and sat him up, and found he wasn't much hurt. The bullet had just scraped across the top of his left shoulder. I have to admit I blew a sigh of relief, because the way he went down it looked like he'd been shot right through the heart—what was left of it, anyway. Chance gritted his teeth and kept up a dark muttering under his breath while Aunt Bertha and I were bandaging him, the gist of which seemed to be that the future didn't look promising for certain parties once he got his hands on them.

In the meanwhile we could hear the cousins thrashing around in the woods and shouting back and forth to each other from so many different places you'd have sworn there was an army of them in there. As we were finishing up with Chance's shoulder we heard them contract into a foursome and head back all together—but when they got into camp they didn't have anybody else with them. Lem said they'd beat a half-mile stretch of woods to a pulp, but the fugitive had beat it back to where he left his horse without taking any of the stops along the way, judging from the looks of the bushes he'd crashed through. All the boys got was some poison oak and the gun. It was a brand-new Winchester and it had been fired recently, but that didn't tell us anything we didn't already know.

Of course Aunt Bertha was mad as heck that they'd let the fellow slip through their fingers, and the cousins weren't any too happy about it themselves. We had a nice scene—Aunt Bertha chewed out Lem, Lem blamed the boys, the boys pointed fingers at each other, et cetera and so forth. You know the way of these little family quarrels.

"Don't get yourselves excited," said Chance when they paused for breath.

Hearing this coming from *him* they all stopped dead and stared at him, completely forgetting what they'd been about to say.

Chance was sitting on the ground looking dark and moody. He said, "It doesn't matter that you didn't catch him. I think we already know who it was."

"We do?" said Lem, who didn't.

Chance looked over at me and I nodded.

"Our friend Mr. Torrance doesn't like long engagements, looks like," I said.

"So what are you going to do about it?" demanded Aunt Bertha.

"I haven't got it thought out yet, but it'll be something worth writing home about, you can bet," said Chance darkly.

"Not you," said Aunt Bertha in disgust. "I wasn't talking to you."

"No," I said, "she wasn't talking to you. We never use that tone of voice on anybody but family."

"For Pete's sake, can't you leave your confounded family out of it for once?" said Chance, and something about the way he said it stopped me cold.

He didn't sound temperamental or cross or excited anymore, just tired, and disappointed and hurt, and I don't mean just in the shoulder. There was a little break in his voice that got to me somehow—you know I was fond of the kid, after all. I think it did the others, too, because they didn't say anything, just looked at each other.

I went over to Chance and put my hand on his shoulder (not the bandaged one, of course; I'm not that dumb). "I'm going to do something about it, and *how*," I said. "First thing in the morning I'm going into town to do a little detective work. I'll get the goods on Roger Torrance if I have to put all of Culver's Corners into footprint casts to do it. You get some rest; you need it. I'll handle everything. You just leave it to me, Chance."

Chapter Fourteen

I Play Detective

I DON'T KNOW why everybody thinks detectives have such a hard time of it. It's kind of like doing a problem in arithmetic—you put two and two together and then look in the back of the book to see if you guessed the answer right.

I'm no mathematical genius, but I figured I could do a little algebraic assumption when I had to. My method was pretty simple. I just rode down the main street of Culver's Corners and turned in at the livery. You see, I knew that x, Roger Torrance didn't own a horse, and y, our bushwhacker had most certainly ridden off on one, so if it was Torrance he'd have to have had z, a livery horse. The logical solution was a little q and a with the livery stable keeper.

The keeper was an acquaintance of mine and didn't suspect me of having any interior motives. Besides which, business was slow, and he was spoiling for something to talk to that didn't have four hoofs and a tail. And did he talk! He was a detective's dream and the worst nightmare of anybody with an alibi. I could have written a monograph on the movements of every horse in Culver's Corners between five o'clock and midnight after listening to him for a quarter of an hour. But when I'd stuck it out through the wheat and the chaff, not to mention the oats, I finally got what I was looking for.

Just as I thought, Roger Torrance had come in the night before about seven o'clock and rented a horse. About two hours later he'd come back with a kind of wild look in his eye, wearing enough greenery in his hair to have gone on as the tree in a Christmas pageant, and looking like he'd been doing all the running instead of the horse. He turned his mount over to the keeper and skedaddled out the back way, looking over his shoulder like he was afraid somebody was still after him. I experienced a very kindly feeling toward my young cousins when I heard that.

So far, so good. I stood there nodding my head with a satisfied smile, like a Scotland Yard inspector right before Sherlock Holmes gives him a dash of cold water. But you know what they say—murder comes out. I guess that goes for attempted murder too. And I helped it along. I suppose beginner's luck had gone to my head so that I went and broke the simple rule that says you should never ask a witness a question you don't already know the answer to.

"And nobody else came in here last night?"

"Nope, nobody. Oh, except for Miss Fayett, of course."

"Miss who?" I echoed, the Scotland-Yard smile fading perceptibly.

"Miss Fayett."

"Miss Meredith Fayett?" I said laboriously, trying to adjust my brain to the fact—as if there'd been at least a half-dozen Miss Fayetts in Culver's Corners.

"Yep. She rode in and left her horse here for a spell while she was seeing somebody in town. Looked kind of flustered—but when she came back later she seemed easier in her mind. I guess that was a quarter of an hour or so before Mr. Torrance came in for his horse."

And while I was wringing the water out of my theory, he added the last drop by saying airily, "He was in here this morning, too. Got a horse half an hour ago. He seems awful fond of riding all of a sudden. Maybe he's taken up hunting," he suggested brightly.

"He has," I said, "and I'm about to."

I left my horse at a hitching rail and walked down the street toward Roger Torrance's office with my head down, thinking hard. I didn't like it. I didn't like it at all. I mean, when a married woman comes into town to see somebody, and a quarter of an hour later somebody goes out of town and tries to make her a widow—well, even dear old Watson would have to admit it looks a little too much like circumstantial evidence for the husband's peace of mind. And Chance didn't have a whole lot of that to spare to begin with.

I'm not sure what I was planning to do when I got to the office, but it was probably something unpleasant and rather illegal. Luckily for me the long arm of coincidence decided to take a hand, which it's often forced to do when the best of detectives have interrogated themselves into a corner. When I was a couple houses away from the office I happened to look up, and immediately dodged into Mrs. Perry's rose-bushes. I'd seen Roger Torrance and Meredith Fayett standing together in front of Torrance's office.

I poked my head up from the bushes and took a cautious inventory. They hadn't seen me. They were still talking earnestly together. Torrance's livery horse and Meredith's own little brown mare that I'd saddled for her many a time were standing together at the hitching rail nearby. I also became aware that I hadn't chosen the best vantage point. It's nearly impossible to eavesdrop from twenty yards away, and it's hard to concentrate on anything when you have a bumblebee hovering about your left ear and a pack of thorns showing their teeth all around you. I kicked against the pricks in an attempt to make them let go of my coat, but they wouldn't, and all I succeeded in doing was mashing Mrs. Perry's petunias underfoot. So I gave up and settled down to watch the culprits in a prickle of anticipation.

Fortunately Roger Torrance was fond of those stage gestures that are meant for the back row of the third balcony, so I was able to follow along pretty well even without the aid of the libretto. He seemed to be trying to convince her of something. Meredith didn't look too sure, but eventually she seemed to change her mind and nodded. There was a short palaver that might have meant anything, and then they went to their horses and mounted, and rode off together.

It made me pretty sick, I can tell you, and good and sore at Meredith Fayett. Here was a fine up-standing young fellow like Chance Stevens breaking his heart in little pieces over her, and there she was fraternizing and co-conspiring with a monumental sneak like Roger Torrance. Roger Torrance!

I waited until they'd turned the corner, and then I backed out of my thicket with only moderate bloodshed, putting a hobnailed stamp on the petunias' death-warrant as I went. The roses were awfully sorry to see me go, judging by the way they tried to hang on to me. I tell you, whatever poet it was that wanted to sleep in a bed of roses ought to have had his head examined.

I didn't have time to go back for my horse; I just wanted to see which road out of town they were taking. I ran around a house, knocked over a pile of crates and scared a couple of alley cats out of their wits. I cut across a backyard and nearly hung myself on Mrs. O'Neal's clothesline, clambered over a fence with a dishtowel still trailing over my shoulder, took a few more twists and turns, and to make a long story short, I crawled out of the culvert by the bridge across the creek just in time to see Meredith and Torrance disappearing around the bend of the road on the far side. Then I went back to town by the civilized route, got my horse and headed for camp.

When I got there the cousins had the horses saddled and the mules hitched up. Aunt Bertha had her hat on and the buggy whip in her hand, which

meant either that she was ready to depart for somewhere or she'd been encouraging them to maintain a
lively pace. Chance was sitting off to one side breaking
a twig into bits, looking about as lonely as the last
Mohican. I heaved a sigh as I swung down from my
horse and went toward him. I wasn't looking forward
to telling him what I had to tell him. My relations
sensed something was up and streamed after me like a
flock of magnets.

Chance jumped up and met me halfway. "What
did you find out, Marty?" he asked quickly.

I heaved another sigh. It's not often I get
theatrical enough for two sighs in one minute, but the
atmosphere of the piece was getting to me, you might
say.

"Sonny boy, I'm afraid I've got bad news for
you," said I. "But just keep in mind life's full of dis-
appointments, and we're all bound to run up against
our share of 'em sooner or —"

"Go on," said Chance impatiently.

"Torrance is the one, all right. He rented a horse
for a woodland jaunt last night and came back with the
hounds after him. But that's not all." I sighed yet again.
"Miss Meredith went into town last night to see
somebody. After she left — *he* left." I waited a second to
let this sink in.

Out of the corner of my eye I saw Aunt Bertha
look at Lem and give a significant grunt, and he didn't
ask why, so I knew the implications were plain
enough.

I said slowly, "I went up to Torrance's office

this morning…and when I got there, I saw—"

"Go on, go on," said Chance, who was a glutton for punishment if there ever was one.

I made an effort. "I saw her there with him. They were talking something over pretty seriously—and then they rode off together. They took the north fork beyond the bridge."

Chance looked down at the ground, and didn't say anything. After a minute he turned and walked away a few steps, and just stood there, looking down. I wished for goodness' sake he'd blow his top or swear or blame me or *something*, and I got so fidgety I began to think of doing something along those lines myself just to break the silence. I was just considering what would happen if I stepped on Lem's foot when Chance swung around to face us with his mouth set in a way that meant something doing. He squared his shoulders and said to Aunt Bertha in a grim and desperate way:

"How would you like to get your ring back?"

Aunt Bertha didn't say anything, but the light of battle flashed in her eye.

"Oh, boy!" said Lem like a kid who's been told he's going to the zoo.

"Oh, boy," I echoed in the voice of one who sees the lions let out of their cages.

Aunt Bertha pounced—figuratively, I'm glad to say. "Marty, if you start griping now I'll—I'll pulverize you. If you don't throw in with us on this—"

"Oh, I'm coming," I said. "Believe you me, I'd like a wholesome crack at Roger Torrance on my own hook, even though it's not *my* wife he's run off with.

He deserves it. I'm with you, Chance, for better or—come what may," I substituted hastily.

Chance was so affected by my loyalty that he blinked a couple of times. "You're an old pal, Marty," he said huskily, so that Lem got a little choked up too. "I knew I could count on you."

Chance took a survey of the troops, and while I don't think the sight would have been encouraging to Grant or McClellan, he seemed satisfied. "Let's go," he said shortly, then spun on his heel and made for his horse, and we marched after him.

CHAPTER FIFTEEN

We Capture the Cabin

COUSIN LEM had his shining hour then. He'd
always been the top tracker of the Second Set
back home, and now Chance and Aunt Bertha
drove him like a pair of impatient coon-hunters with
one very nervous bloodhound. He'd swapped his seat
on the rig for one of the boys' horses, and he hung so
far down one side of its neck you'd have sworn he was
trying to touch his nose to the ground, but this was
mostly a show to convince them he was really doing
something. Lem could practically read sign with his
eyes shut. Once we were out on the north road he
struck the trail easy, and followed it a couple of miles
to where it left the main road and took a narrow little
path that twisted back and forth up into the hills.
When we'd got this far we didn't really need him
anymore, because both Chance and I had a pretty good
idea where they were heading. Years back some old
hunter had built a little cabin up against the side of a

hill, and though it was still used by a hunter or a drifting cowpuncher now and then, mostly people stopped there when they were out riding for pleasure, to eat a picnic lunch or just so they could say they'd stopped at the old hunter's cabin. It sounded like the kind of place a Roger Torrance sort would take a girl on an outing.

I thought that old buckboard would be shaken to pieces before we got to the top of the hill. Half the time the trail wasn't much more than a narrow rain-washed gully, so the wheels were always halfway up the bank on one side or the other. Whenever the trail widened a little the rig would shriek and rattle and bounce up on the other side and then repeat the whole performance. Aunt Bertha hung onto the lines and growled at the mules, and the kid on the seat next to her hung on for dear life as the rig swayed and jolted back and forth. For all this they kept up pretty well with us on horseback, and we were all together when we sighted the cabin on the slope above us.

Nobody was in sight but there were some horses standing in front of it. Chance pulled up and slid off his horse and the rest of us followed suit, though Aunt Bertha had got into an argument with the mules and stayed on the seat.

Now, Lem's method would have been to melt into the woods and kind of trickle in around the place so that you'd never have known we were there until we helped ourselves to a chair in the parlor. Not Chance. He just started straight up the last bit of hill on foot and the cousins followed him looking as hypnotized as a forlorn hope.

Just about then I thought I heard a confused noise coming from the cabin, and Roger Torrance came out the door in kind of a hurry. At sight of him my cousins gave the tally-ho-and-have-at-him cry and hit that slope like it was Bunker Hill, and the horses by the cabin scattered in all directions like somebody had thrown a firecracker in the middle of them.

For the first time in my life I was glad I came of a family of lunatics. When Torrance saw who was rushing at him (rifles in hand) he got all big around the eyes and white around the gills and started backing up stiffly, too scared even to run. I suppose it didn't help matters to see Chance Stevens leading the charge after he'd gone to all the trouble of assassinating him just a few hours before. As for me, I was sure Chance was going to kill him, and I knew I was too far behind to do anything about it, and I was already thinking out my testimony about extenuating circumstances.

He didn't, though. When he got to Torrance he just took a handful of tie and waistcoat and starched shirt-collar in his left and let go one good, solid driving punch with his right. It was a real beauty. Torrance laid down flat on his back and didn't get up, and the boys all stood around and looked down at him like he was a rare curiosity. I think they had a lot more respect for Chance after that.

The next thing I knew Meredith came running out of the cabin, all excited and out of breath, crying out "Chance! Oh, Chance!" fit to melt a heart of stone.

I don't know what was up with his heart, but

there was a stone on Chance's mind all right—a green one. It's a cinch Meredith wouldn't have stopped, but when she got to him he caught her firmly by both arms and stopped her. He took hold of her left wrist and pulled Grandma's ring off her finger.

"What are you doing?" cried Meredith. "Here! wait!—that's my wedding-ring. Give it back!"

"What for?" said Chance. "So you can use it for collateral to hire some more bushwhackers next time you want to get out of a deal? I don't think so. Let me tell you something, Meredith Stevens—up till now this ring has been used for honorable marriages. But I guess I was wrong about you—seems you don't know what honorable means, so I don't think you're fit to wear it."

Meredith could only gasp.

"Lem!" said Chance sharply. Lem gave notice of his presence, and up came Chance's hand with the ring in it. My heart did a combination hop-skip-and-jump as the stone of contention went spinning through the air like a bright green daytime shooting star. But Lem caught it safely and the boys raised a hair-raising cheer as he hustled down the hill to hand it over to Aunt Bertha.

Meredith pulled away from Chance. I could tell she was angry, but her eyes were sparkling with tears and her chin trembled a little. She had some spunk, did that girl. She was too proud to try and make explanations and excuses like most girls would have done. She turned her back on him and marched off down the slope, trying hard to keep him from seeing how close to crying she was. She brushed past Lem, who shuffled back a few steps and tried to look like it wasn't *his* fault, and went right up to the buckboard and spoke to Aunt Bertha (which took some courage in itself) in a voice that shook just a little bit. "May I ride back to town with you, please? My horse has run away and I don't want to wait until *somebody* has time to catch it."

I winced. Even a sweet, pretty girl like Meredith Fayett, when she thinks she's been ill-used, can make ordinary sentences bite until you feel like you're holding a double handful of ice cubes and can't find anywhere to put them down.

Aunt Bertha is always on the women's side when it isn't a family matter, so she moved over right away and made room for Meredith on the seat, shooting a dark look at Chance as she did it, and when Meredith was up beside her she touched up the mules and the rig creaked off.

"Let's take a look around this place," said Chance, who either didn't give a hang about it or did a good job of pretending he didn't.

I followed him without my heart really being in it. Somehow the last scene had dampened my spirits, though I didn't know why. I don't know what I'd been expecting to happen, but still…

Chance went around the back of the cabin while I stepped through the door and took a look inside. There was nothing much but a table, a few chairs, and a closet in the corner.

I was about to turn and go out when all of a

sudden the closet doorknob jiggled.

Doorknobs don't usually jiggle by themselves, so I was intrigued. I stopped to watch and see if this one would do it again.

It did.

The closet had a lock, and the lock had a skeleton key sticking in it, and I turned it. The door swung open and out tumbled our old friend, the Justice of the Peace.

CHAPTER SIXTEEN

How the Justice of the Peace Was Taken for a Ride

G OOD GRACIOUS me!" gasped the Justice of the Peace.

"Took the words right out of my mouth," said I. "Hey, Chance! Come look what I found."

Chance came in with Lem behind him, and when he saw the little old gent his shoulders kind of slumped again. I think he'd hoped he was through with living reminders.

"What's he doing here?" he said.

"Search me. I found him locked up in the closet for safekeeping."

"Good *gracious* me," said the J. of the P., who'd found a crumpled handkerchief in his pocket and was dabbing away at his head. "Is she all right? I was rather worried, you know — all that dreadful noise outside! — it quite unnerved me. I may have had to do it, though I'm not sure it would have been legal. I'm sure I *hope* it wouldn't! I must look that up when I get home. Good gracious!"

"What's he talking about?" said Chance, utterly bewildered (and I couldn't blame him). Lem was staring at the J. of the P. in a fascinated way, as something entirely new in his experience.

"Why, I have *never*," said the J., puffing up in that official way of his, "in all my years on the bench, performed a marriage ceremony in which a party was unwilling. Especially a lady. But in peril of my life, what could I do?"

A lightning bolt hit me. (Figuratively.) I seized the J. by the collar and he let out a yelp, probably thinking he was in peril of his life again.

"Talk," I ordered. "Begin at the beginning. Try to tell it in order. End your sentences with full stops, and don't stop until you've made some sense. *What really happened here today?*"

Leaving out all the J.'s puffings and gaspings and good-gracious-me-ings, this is what had happened:

Early that morning when the Justice of the Peace was sitting at his desk engaged in his customary occupations (or so he told us), a man appeared in the doorway and asked if he (the Justice, not the man) was the Justice of the Peace. The J. admitted to the charge and the man explained that he'd come from a farm west of town where they were all set to have a wedding, but at the last minute got word that the minister was sick and couldn't come. They wanted the Judge to hustle out and hitch them up before the wedding-cake got stale and the wedding-guests got bored and went home, and they'd pay him double the usual fee.

"I have not been accustomed to travel to perform ceremonies," said the J. of the P. to the man, "but perhaps in this case I might make an exception—"

"Are you coming or ain't you?" said the man, direct and to the point.

"Are you from west of town?" queried the J. incidentally. "I have a sister who lives out that way. I don't believe I know you. Are you a newcomer?"

The man said he wasn't, then said he was, then changed the subject. Was the J. of the P. coming or wasn't he?

The Judge couldn't remember whether he said he was or he wasn't, but the man must have persuaded him, for next thing he knew they were outside and there were horses waiting. The J. balked a little at riding one—he wasn't what you'd call an active gent—but the man boosted him up into the saddle before he even had time to say "Good gracious me."

He was so busy trying to stay in the middle of the horse's back (my deduction, not his; he kind of brushed over this part) that it wasn't till they'd taken the north fork that he noticed anything not according to schedule. "Excuse me," said the old gent politely, "I may be mistaken, but—haven't we missed our way somewhere? I thought—"

The man turned and just kind of looked him over, then turned the other way and spit out his tobacco before answering, "We'll get there."

The J.'s anxieties had arisen (I think that's how

he put it) and he was about to register further protest,
but at that moment he espied (his word, not mine) a
most fearsome-looking weapon on the person of his
conductor—which I took to mean a Colt—and judged
it prudent to hold his tongue. So there wasn't any
conversation between when he reached this verdict
and when they reached the hunters' cabin. The J.
brushed over the ride up the hill, too.

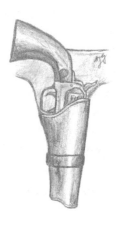

As he'd kind of suspected, there wasn't any
wedding in progress at the cabin, just a table and some
chairs and a closet in the corner. The man planted the J.
in a chair and told him he was to act natural. Then he
clammed up and didn't speak for a quarter of an hour,
and the J. of the P. sat and tried to act natural till his
head ached, until finally they heard some more horses
outside.

The hoofbeats stopped and after a minute the
Justice heard some voices. He craned his neck a little

and managed to see through the half-open door that it was Meredith Fayett and Roger Torrance, standing together and looking at the view from the hill. Torrance was leaning kind of close to her and speaking in a romantically lowered voice.

"Only imagine, Meredith," he was saying, "if all our troubles were over; if there were no more obstacles in our way—if we could be married at this moment. With no more delays—"

"Roger," said Meredith in a small voice, "there's something I've been meaning to tell—"

At this moment the Justice of the Peace sneezed. They couldn't blame him for that; he'd been told to act natural and you can't get any more natural than that.

"Why, there's somebody else here already!" said Roger Torrance hastily. "Let's see who it is. Why, it's the Judge!"

The J. of the P. welcomed them to his humble abode as politely as he could, all things considered. Torrance was as merry as a marriage bell but somehow forgot to introduce the judge-napper, who stood in the corner of the room with his arms folded, as silent as somebody's footman. The J. saw Meredith steal a curious glance at the man, and tried telegraphing to her with his eyes that all was not as natural as it seemed. But all he did was catch the eye of the man in the corner, which wasn't pleasant.

"What a *coincidence*," said Torrance, placing another chair for Meredith to sit down on, "that it should be you. We were speaking—or thinking—of you just a moment ago."

"*Were* you?" said the J., with one eye on the man in the corner.

"Well, of an occasion coming up," said Torrance, "when we'll be needing your services." He sort of aimed this remark in Meredith's direction.

"Oh," said Meredith, trying to smile, but it wasn't her usual one. The J. observed that she wasn't acting quite natural herself. Like she was thinking of something—or someone—else.

"Sooner than later, I hope," said Roger Torrance, making Romeo eyes at her. I think he would have had hold of her hand by now if it wasn't for the mixed company.

"Good gracious, I think not," said the J. of the P. "The marriage laws are such—as I was explaining to you last evening, Miss Fayett—"

"Last when?" said Torrance.

"I went to see the Judge last night," said Meredith, turning pink—I could easily picture it when the J. said so. "There were a few things I wanted to be clear about."

"Yes. We discussed this very question, the amount of time required for annulment proceedings, which I was happy to inform her is quite lengthy," said the J. of the P. happily indeed. Legal talk was bread and meat and tranquilizer to him. He'd already forgotten the man in the corner for the moment.

"Happy!" said Roger Torrance. His prefabricated smile kind of clattered to the floor, but he gathered it up and pasted it back on. "Why, Judge—"

"Wait, please," said Meredith in an even smaller voice than the one she had used outside. "There—there's something I've got to tell you, Roger. I—I'm beginning to realize I've been very foolish."

She smiled at him shamefacedly, so the Justice said, but looking relieved too. "I am glad we met the Judge, otherwise I don't know how I would have told you. I was trying to think of a way all the way up here."

"Tell me what?" said Roger Torrance, who for once in his life had no idea what was coming next.

Meredith took a deep breath. "When I married Chance Stevens," she said, "it didn't mean anything to me. All I wanted was to keep the ranch. Even afterwards, I only thought of Chance as a good friend, and I took him for granted at that. But when I heard he was dead—I was crushed. I realized all at once how much I'd come to…to care for him—but it was too late. Oh, I was simply miserable. Then when you began coming around, and were so kind to me, I suppose I was grateful to you for making me feel a little better. For being a friend. So when you asked me to marry you, I thought that was enough. I thought I couldn't ever be truly happy again now Chance was gone, so it didn't matter that I might not be perfectly happy with you. I was just in a hurry to try and forget.

"And then Chance came home—and as soon as I saw him I knew what a fool I'd been. It seems terribly unfair to you, Roger—if it wasn't for my actually being *married* to Chance already I don't know if I could bring myself to treat you this badly. But we are married, you see, and—it wouldn't be fair to either you or me, you know, if I married you without really loving you. Please try to understand. I just can't do it. Even if I never saw Chance again, I just—just couldn't marry anybody else as long as he was alive."

It took Roger Torrance several minutes and a lot of swallowing and gulping to recover from this. The way I see it, Meredith's confession hit him like a bolt out of the blue. He'd expected trouble from Chance, but he was so full up with conceit he'd never thought it possible for a girl to like anybody better than him.

Maybe he still hadn't got the idea through his head. If he had, maybe he could have chosen a better answer than the one he finally blurted out.

He said, "But Meredith, Chance Stevens *is* dead. He was killed last night in a—an accident."

Really a brilliant inspiration on his part, that last, but some women are naturally suspicious and Meredith's suspicions were aroused.

"What kind of accident?" she said. All the color had gone out of her face.

Torrance opened his mouth wide, but for once he couldn't get anything to come out of it.

"It wasn't an accident," breathed Meredith. She got up and came at him, and Torrance began making tracks with the moccasins reversed, if you know what I mean. The J. said he'd never seen anything like Meredith's face, all white, and with her big eyes flashing fire as she closed in on him. "*You* did it! You had something to do with it—you've killed him!"

Torrance made a vague denial with his hands,

but kept backing up until he hit the wall. The J. thought Meredith was going to fly at him and personally spoil his complexion, but somehow at the last minute she controlled herself. She picked up her gloves and quirt and turned to the Justice, still shaking with anger. "Judge, will you come back to town with me? I want you to swear out a warrant for that man's arrest."

She turned to go and the J. gladly got up to follow, but 'that man' recovered himself awful quickly and got in the door and blocked them. He'd left off with the smile and charm and he was a lot less scrupulous without them. "No, you don't. You're going to marry me right here and now!"

"I will not!" said Meredith, stamping her foot. "Let me pass!"

"Yes, you will! What do you think I brought you up here for? You get back in there and Judge, you'll perform the ceremony."

"Brought me up here for!" cried Meredith. "To marry you? Did you really think you could get me to do a thing like that—only *hours* after Chance was killed —even if I *didn't* love him? You—you *snake!*"

That made up for just about everything she'd done wrong in my opinion. I only wish I'd been there to hear it.

The J. of the P. was so affected by the argument that followed that he was nearly overcome with emotion in trying to describe it. In a word, Torrance threatened, Meredith refused and the Judge trembled. If Torrance could have coerced Meredith it's a cinch

the old gent would have caved in and married them, if
he hadn't already collapsed by that time. But he was
saved the necessity of doing either by the man in the
corner, who'd gone outside during the argument and
come back again, interrupting with the statement,

"Some people coming."

Meredith bolted for the door, but Torrance
caught her by the arm. She put up a good fight, but he
dragged her back and pushed her into the other
fellow's hands. The J. of the P. was debating within
himself (or so he told us) whether to go to her aid or
run for help, when Roger Torrance pounced on him
and stuffed him in the closet, and there he remained
through the rest of the ordeal, in fear and trembling at
the horrible noises he was hearing outside, until I let
him out.

Right here I'd better add what more I know of
Roger Torrance, because I won't have time in a minute.
He was never quite the same after his second brush
with avenging Fate in the shape of Chance and the
cousins. When we hauled him up before the law over
the little matter of taking that pot-shot at Chance, he
sort of came unraveled and a few more interesting facts
spilled out of him. It seems the mail-order habit had
caught up with our surveyor to the point that if he'd
been monarch of all he surveyed he couldn't have sold
it for enough to get him out of the red. Consequently
there was a lot to be said for the notion of marrying a
pretty young widow with a comfortable bank account
and hiding behind her when the Montgomery Ward
agent showed up on the doorstep. Anyway, the law

said what it thought, which was a lot, and Roger Torrance went where all villains go when they're no longer necessary to the plot.

As for the other fellow, Meredith told me afterwards that when he saw what happened to Torrance by way of the front window, he let go of her and took a flying leap through the back one. We never heard who he was or what happened to him. I think he may be running still.

CHAPTER SEVENTEEN

Chance Issues
Two Invitations

I'VE PURPOSELY kept from trying to describe Chance's looks while the J. of the P. was telling this tale, because I'd have had to wear out a whole Dictionary of Adjectives doing it. When it was over, he turned to me with an expression I don't think I *could* have found a word for even with a thesaurus. But I knew what it meant all right.

As for me, I let out a yell that beat my cousins all hollow and left me hoarse for a week. And then we shot out the door in this order: Chance, me, Lem, and the Justice of the Peace, who didn't exactly want to come but had to, as Lem was dragging him by the collar. Chance flung himself into the saddle and spurred his horse recklessly down the hill, and I wasn't far behind him. Lem picked up the J. by a leg and an arm and hurled him onto the back of one of the boys' horses by main force, clambered on another one himself and they took out after us. I guess Lem didn't want to miss the show but he didn't want to let a novelty like the Justice slip through his fingers either. The boys just stood and stared.

I'll brush over the ride down the hill. All you need to know is that we got to the bottom and got there alive. When we hit the main road, there was the buckboard a quarter of a mile ahead, going at a trot. I swear I could see the mules' ears bobbing even at that distance. At first I thought that meant we were getting closer, but after a few minutes I realized that we didn't seem to be gaining on them at all. We were going at a round gallop but still that buckboard hung just out of reach. Finally it dawned on me—the mules were running away, and making a thorough job of it as usual. They'd heard us coming up behind and decided it was a race. I think Chance realized it at the same time I did, because he started using the rein-ends on his horse, front and back, like he was coming down to the wire in the Kentucky Derby. I stayed right with him and boy, did we give Lem and the Justice a run for their money. I could hear the Justice yipping and howling for mercy behind me for most of the way.

Then we came in sight of the turn towards town. The road up till there was flat and straight and smooth as silk, just the kind that runaways love. Aunt Bertha was some driver, but I doubt Ben-Hur himself could have held in that pair of mules on that stretch of road. And there was that sharp-right turn rimmed round with bushes, and I knew the mules were going to make that turn, but the buckboard wasn't, and we could never get there in time to stop it. All we could do was watch. Chance gave a choked, frustrated cry as they came up on the turn.

It sure must have been the hand of Providence that pulled the pin out of the clevis as they took that corner, because there wasn't any earthly reason for it to have come out. The mules went on their merry way dragging the doubletree behind them, and the buckboard slid neatly into the bushes with a slithering crash.

When we got there a few seconds later, Meredith and Aunt Bertha were still up on the seat, struggling with the branches around them. Chance made a flying dismount he hasn't equaled since and practically pulled Meredith down from the buckboard. "Are you all right?" he shouted at her.

"Yes!" she flung back a bit petulantly. I mean, when you've just been run away with, sling-shot into a hedge and are still trying to pick leaves out of your hair, that's not the time you want to be answering questions with obvious answers.

Once Chance had convinced himself she was telling the truth he turned around and looked up at Aunt Bertha. "Ma'am, I've made an awful mistake," he said. "When you get right down to it you folks have been pretty darn good to me, and I don't want to be the cause of bringing trouble on your family."

"Hey?" said Aunt Bertha, plainly mystified.

Lem and I, who had got down off our horses by this time, paused to listen. The J. of the P. had adhered himself to his saddle horn with both hands and sat there vibrating in the background.

"The ring," said Chance. "Your grandmother's wedding-ring. I made a mistake giving it back to you. Do you know what's going to happen when you take that thing home? Chaos. Terror and tragedy. Everybody wants a finger in the pie, but that thing's only big enough for one finger. You let that go on much longer and things are bound to turn really ugly. Look at the facts, ma'am. You've got to ditch it now—get it out of the family before it's too late."

I never in my life saw anything like the sight of Chance Stevens standing there by the wrecked buckboard, trying to convince Aunt Bertha the formidable old veteran of a thousand squabbles to close the book on a thirty-years' family feud, all the while with a pleading little-boy look in his eyes that said he was really asking for something else.

Aunt Bertha glanced toward Meredith, and looked at Chance again. I saw him mouth the word "please."

She began to fumble ponderously with her reticule. Maybe she didn't look much like an angel sitting up aloft, did my Aunt Bertha, perched on the seat of that crazy rig with her old hat over one ear, her hair all awry and leaves sticking all over her, but that's what she must have looked like to Chance just then. "I suppose you're right," she said just as sourly as ever. "This old thing's been a tarnation and a curse to the family long enough. Time our luck had a change. You take it and get rid of it—if you can."

She held out Grandma's ring.

If we had been in a play, or a book, I think Lem

and I would have uttered a gasp and clutched at each other for support, and both of us probably would have gone down anyway. As it was we just stared dumbly with our mouths wide open.

Chance took it, turned around and faced Meredith, who had been standing there watching everything, not really understanding it but interested in spite of herself. He held out Grandma's ring to her.

"It's yours, if you want it," he said. "The Judge told me everything. I was a fool. But if you don't mind that, then—you can have me too, because I'm all yours already, if you know what I mean. If not"—he swallowed hard—"just say the word and I'll let you go to—to do whatever you want."

Meredith looked a long while at the ring in his hand, shining bright green in the sunlight. Then she looked up at his face, and back at the ring, and at his face again, and she saw that he really meant it...and then she gave a little cry and flung herself into his arms, and he held her tight, and—

Well, that ought to be the end of the story. But

there are a couple more things left to be told.

Aunt Bertha may have had a change of heart, but even that wasn't enough to shake the earth so that it could be felt down in Arkansas, so we had to communicate with the rest of the family by post. Aunt Bertha was dictator and Lem was dictated-to, and between them they spoiled a ream of paper before they got a satisfactory letter written—although Lem had the nerve to say that if it wasn't for Chance and Meredith and me chiming in with our suggestions all the time they would have got done a lot faster. But it was written, and stamped, and sent, and in time we got an answer. Several answers. You wouldn't expect *my* family to agree on something right off the bat, would you? Of course not. Aunt Bertha fired off another letter and back came another salvo of replies, which was pretty much like a long-distance family meeting, come to think of it. We had a few meetings of our own up in Missouri, and I'll bet there was one continuous one down in Arkansas all the time this was going on.

In the end there came a day when Lem came charging out of the post-office at Culver's Corners with a yell like an Indian throwing tea overboard in Boston Harbor, waving an envelope in one hand and a letter in the other, and we all crowded around demanding to see it and what was in it and telling each other to be quiet so we could hear.

Aunt Bertha read it slowly, frowning hard. "They say," she began deliberately, "that they've agreed to call it quits over the ring if—"

"What'd I tell you?" said Chance jubilantly.

"IF," repeated Aunt Bertha, "if — where was I?"

"'Certain conditions,' " said Lem, who was reading over her shoulder.

"Conditions? What conditions?" said Meredith, pushing past Chance to have a look. Oh, she was there too. You couldn't get hold of one without the other those days. I tell you, they behaved more like schoolyard sweethearts than people who've been married going on half a year. His arm was always around her like it grew there, and you could hardly get her to listen to anything unless he was saying it.

"They'd like to meet Meredith, and Chance, and get the story straight, because nobody understands it yet and they've worn out the letters passing them around," said Aunt Bertha, condensing as she read, "so as soon as they can agree on who's to come, and Uncle Tom has sold a cow to pay for railroad fare, they're coming up here —"

Lem let out a kind of yowl.

"What's the matter with you?" I asked.

"I didn't read that far," he said.

"Coming here," finished Aunt Bertha, "for a visit."

"Suffering second cousins," said I *sotto voce*.

"Be quiet, Marty," said Aunt Bertha, folding up the letter. "Insanely curious, that's what they are. It runs in that branch of the family. They've already made up their minds, of course."

"Of course," said Chance, and winked at me.

"We'll stay till they get here," began Aunt Bertha.

"That could be a while," said Lem dubiously, "'cause it's haying time down home, you know. And we've got nowhere to stay since we got evicted from the boarding-house this morn..." Aunt Bertha gave him a look, and he kind of trailed off.

"Evicted? Why?" said Meredith.

"Partly because we haven't got any money left. But partly because that old man named Foster down the street told Mrs. Harvey some extraordinary story about you, Marty, wallowing in somebody's rosebushes and running headfirst into a wall. He says he saw it from his upstairs window. Mrs. Harvey believes in heredity," said Aunt Bertha.

"It wasn't a wall, it was a pile of crates that shouldn't have been there in the first place," said I.

Chance and Meredith exchanged a look. Quick as I was, I couldn't translate it. They had a language all their own these days.

"We're a little short-handed at the ranch," said Chance.

I gave him a look that ought to have knocked him over backwards. "I've stood by you through thick and thin and matrimony," said I in as deeply wounded a tone as I could muster, "and you're going to repay me by inflicting my relations on me?"

"Oh, shut up," said Chance amiably. "If it wasn't for you and your relations—"

"If it wasn't for me and my relations," said I, "you'd be short a wife right now. Don't you forget that, sonny boy."

And of course he couldn't answer that.

"We don't inflict on anybody," said Lem indignantly. "We'll earn our keep, won't we, Ma?"

"They can cook," I admitted.

"They'll do more than cook if I have anything to do with it," said Aunt Bertha, and the boys shivered a little. "You don't charge us for board and we don't charge you for our work, and everybody'll come out square. You never made a better deal."

"Well, I don't know about *that*," said Meredith, smiling up at Chance as she linked her arm through his. All's well that ends with a smile, somebody said once, and while I don't know how true that is, it certainly seemed that way when it was Meredith smiling. Maybe it *is* true. I know Chance would agree with me, anyway. As I was telling my godson the other day (young Marty Stevens, don't you know—great kid), it's the little things that count after all.

"So can we stay?" said Lem anxiously.

"We'd be delighted to have you," said Meredith firmly, and that was that, because she was the last word around that place, let me tell *you!*

It purely amazed me, by the way, how well Meredith and Aunt Bertha got on together. They were the last two women in the world I'd have thought would have anything in common, but they were friends even before the mules had pitched them into the hedge. It just goes to show you that in one respect all women are alike. I don't think any man has found out what it is yet, but there's no getting away from it.

"There's nothing saying *you've* got to stay, Marty," said Aunt Bertha. "We can get along very well without you. One less mouth to feed, anyway," she added.

"Did I say I didn't want to stay?" I demanded in a hurry. "Ask Chance. I didn't say that, Chance, did I?"

I turned to Chance, but he wasn't there. I looked around and saw him standing a little ways off with Meredith. They were standing close together and her face was turned up toward his and they were saying all kinds of sentimental things to each other in a low voice that made me blush to hear them. But my relations all stood there with their eyes and ears wide open, perfectly delighted. I suppose it was latent to that branch of the family.

And that's all, except that about a week later I was working out in the ranch yard when Aunt Bertha came to the back door and called me over to the house to show me something. She'd been helping Meredith with the housework and gone to fetch something from a bureau, and had opened the wrong drawer by mistake, and what do you think she found?

Why, it was an old hat that had been in the water and was somewhat the worse for it, and was all shot full of holes besides. And it didn't take a deductionist to tell how it had come in that drawer, or that its business there had been to be taken out and cried over every so often during those weeks when poor little Meredith presumed Chance to be in the same condition as the hat.

"You know what still beats me?" I said, scratching my head. "If she had the nerve to ask him to marry her, why in burning blazes couldn't she just up and tell him that she loved him?"

But Aunt Bertha merely gave me a look that said plain as plain that I didn't know anything about women, and went back in the house.

ABOUT THE AUTHOR

ELISABETH GRACE FOLEY (that's Elisabeth spelled with an S, mind you) has been an insatiable reader and eager history buff ever since she learned to read, and has been scribbling stories ever since she learned to write. She now combines those interests in writing historical fiction. Her short Western novel *Left-Hand Kelly* was a nominee for the 2015 Peacemaker Award for Best Independently-Published Western Novel. She is also the author of the historical-mystery series The Mrs. Meade Mysteries; a series of fairytale-retelling novellas set in different historical eras; and a variety of short fiction. Her work has appeared online at *Rope and Wire* and *The Western Online*. When not reading or writing, she enjoys music, crocheting, spending time outdoors, and watching sports and classic film. She lives in upstate New York with her family and the world's best German Shepherd. Visit her online at

www.elisabethgracefoley.com

Made in the USA
Las Vegas, NV
07 October 2024